Alice's Adventchers
in Wunderland

Alice's Adventchers in Wunderland

By

Lewis Carroll

ILLUSTRATED BY

JOHN TENNIEL

TRANSLATED INTO SCOUSE BY

MARVIN R. SUMNER

evertype

2015

Published by Evertype, 73 Woodgrove, Ballyfin Road, Portlaoise, Co. Laois, R32 ENP6, Ireland. *www.evertype.com*.

Original title: *Alice's Adventures in Wonderland*.
First edition 2015.
A catalogue record for this book is available from the British Library.

ISBN-10 1-78201-107-2
ISBN-13 978-1-78201-107-1

Typeset in De Vinne Text, Mona Lisa, ENGRAVERS' ROMAN, and *Liberty* by Michael Everson.

Illustrations: John Tenniel, 1865.

Cover: Michael Everson.

Printed by LightningSource.

Foreword

$\mathcal{L}$ewis Carroll is a pen-name: Charles Lutwidge Dodgson was the author's real name and he was lecturer in Mathematics in Christ Church, Oxford. Dodgson began the story on 4 July 1862, when he took a journey in a rowing boat on the river Thames in Oxford together with the Reverend Robinson Duckworth, with Alice Liddell (ten years of age) the daughter of the Dean of Christ Church, and with her two sisters, Lorina (thirteen years of age), and Edith (eight years of age). As is clear from the poem at the beginning of the book, the tree girls asked Dodgson for a story and reluctantly at first he began to tell the first version of the story to them. There are many half-hidden references made to the five of them throughout the text of the book itself, which was published finally in 1865.

"Scouse" is the name of the unique dialect of English spoken in Liverpool. It is a relatively new dialect, dating to the 19th century, showing some influence of speakers from England, Scotland, Wales, and Ireland. The Beatles are perhaps the most famous speakers of Scouse, or at least the first speakers who came to public prominence outside the Liverpool region. Following this Foreword is a brief sketch of the orthographic principles used in presenting the Liverpudlian dialect in this edition.

The Scouse translation was first prepared by Marvin R. Sumner in 1990, as part of the "Alice 125" celebration organized in Australia. A number of new translations were inspired by that project, but for a variety of reasons, some—or most—of them were never published. The first of them which *did* see the light of day was the Tongan *Alice*.[1] It is my great pleasure and honour to be able to bring out at long last this Scouse translation in time for the "Alice 150" celebrations being held this year. My thanks are due to June Lornie for putting me in touch with Marvin, and to Marvin for allowing me to publish his translation.

Just before publication, Marvin related to me the following

> As you no doubt already know, Lewis Carroll once lived at Daresbury, not more than a short carriage ride from Liverpool. I feel he is an honourary "Scouser" and his lively wit would have nade him a "dockyard bard", especially so in describing schooling and teachers in the Mock Turtle's story. Straightforward Docker's humour!

Carroll was familiar with dialect writing, of course, and wrote some of it himself. I wager he'd have approved of Alice in a Scouse Wonderland.

Michael Everson
Portlaoise, July 2015

---

1 Carroll, Lewis. 2014. *'Alisi 'i he Fonua 'o e Fakaofo'*. Translated into Tongan by Siutāula Cokeer and Telesia Kalavite. Cathair na Mart: Evertype. ISBN 978-1-78201-062-3

On Dialect Orthography

$\mathcal{P}$ublishing text in an unstandardized orthography is a challenge. A balance must be found between faithfulness to the sounds of the dialect and legibility to an audience who reads the standard language. English dialect spellings are nothing new, of course: from Robert Louis Stevenson's representation of Scots in *Kidnapped* to Mark Twain's representation of Missouri dialect in his *Adventures of Huckleberry Finn* various approaches have been taken. Often these approaches make use of what is known as "the apologetic apostrophe" to mark letters from the standard language which have been "dropped". In the case of Scouse, another feature, known as "eye dialect" is often found in dialect literature. This has been largely avoided here. Most dialect literature, whether poetry or prose, is fairly short and eye-dialect doesn't necessarily confuse the reader. But in a 27,000-word novel, the representation of *Queen* as *Kween* (where there is arguably no pronunciation difference),[2] or re-spelling words for re-spelling's sake (should the Duchess put her arm around Alice's *waste* rather than her *waist?*)

---

2 Initial /k/ is strongly aspirated in Scouse and so this word can be [kʰwiːn] even [kˣwiːn], but the letter *k* doesn't imply this vis à vis *q*.

ultimately makes the text harder to read, when instead the salient phonetic and grammatical features of the dialect are what is of interest. Here, we write *know/knew* rather than *now/new*, *continued* rather than *kontinyewed*, and *mentioned* rather than *menshuned*, rather following the Scots model, where a literary orthography differs from the standard language where necessary, but retains familiar word-shapes where possible. This practice was recognized in the 1947 Scots Style Sheet and the 1985 Recommendations for Writers in Scots, both of which discourage the apologetic apostrophe while retaining it for ordinary purposes. Many of these recommendations apply easily to the linguistic features of Scouse, and have been followed in the text used in this book. In the Evertype editions of *Alice* in Appalachian English[3] and Cornu-English,[4] the spellings used were regularized on similar literary orthographical grounds.

Since the reader may appreciate a summary of the orthographic conventions used here for the Scouse dialect, a list is given below.

- Words ending in *-ing* have been spelled as *-in*; participles in *-en* have been retained: *writin* 'writing', *written* 'written'; words derived from *-thing* have been spelled *-tin*: *sometin* 'something'.
- The final apostrophe is not used: *an* 'and' is used instead of *an'*; *em* 'them' is used instead of *'em*; *o* 'of' is used instead of *o'*.
- Before a vowel *o* is written *of*: compare *one o dem* 'one of them' and *one of ers* 'one of hers'.

---

3 Carroll, Lewis. 2012. *Alice's Adventures in an Appalachian Wonderland*. Translated into Appalatchan Dialeck by Byron W. Sewell an Victoria J. Sewell. Pitchures after John Tenniel by Byron W. Sewell. Cathair na Mart: Evertype. ISBN 978-1-78201-010-4
4 Carroll, Lewis. 2015. *Alice's Ventures in Wunderland*. Translated into Cornu-English by Alan M. Kent. Cathair na Mart: Evertype. ISBN 978-1-78201-102-6

- The words *he*, *his*, *him*, *her*, *it*, *they*, *their*, and *them* are written *e*, *iz*, *im*, *er*, *it*, *dey*, *deir*, and *dem*.
- Initial *h-* is dropped in *ave* 'have', *ad* 'had', and their derivatives, and generally, as in *Atter* 'Hatter', *er* 'her', *oo* 'who', *ouse* 'house'; *h-* is kept orthographically when silent (*honest*, *hour*) or when sounded in the standard language (*hm*).
- Initial *wh-* is retained although the pronunciation is [w] not [ʌ].
- The merger of the vowel of "fur" (RP [fɜ:]) with the vowel in "fair" ([fɛ:]) is indicated by spellings like *berd* 'bird', *ferst* 'first', *lerned* 'learned', *terned* 'turned', *werd* 'word', and *werse* 'worse'.
- The fricative *th* is becomes *t* [θ > t] when voiceless and *d* [ð > d] when voiced (*tink* 'think', *truw* 'through', *mout* 'mouth', *dat* 'that', *radder* 'rather', *wid* 'with').
- Contractions of the negative particle are treated in two ways. In monosyllables which end in a glottal stop, *n't* is written: *ain't* [ɛnʔ] 'ain't', *caan't* [kˣɑ:nʔ] 'can't', *din't* [dɪnʔ] 'didn't'; but in others where the stop is lost *'n* is used: *do'n* [dɛʉn], *wo'n* [wɛʉn]; in polysyllables the syllabic nasal is also written *'n*: *ad'n* [ædn̩] 'hadn't', *is'n* [ɪzn̩] 'isn't', *was'n* [wəzn̩] 'wasn't', *could'n* [kʊdn̩], *should'n* [ʃʊdn̩], *would'n* [wʊdn̩].
- Final *-st* is often pronounced *-ss*; orthographically, "must" is written *muss* before consonants and in absolute final position, but *must* before vowels: *muss be*, *must ave*.
- Final *-nt* is often pronounced *-n*; orthographically, "went" is written *went* [wɛnʔ] before consonants, but *wenn* [wɛn] before vowels: *went down*, *wenn on*.
- Words in Scouse which have a short *oo* [ʊ] in the standard language have a long one [u:] in Scouse; these are written with *uw* here (*buwk* 'book', *cuwk* 'cook', *luwk*

'look', *shuwk* 'shook'). The graph *uw* is also used in *truw* 'through' (because *trough* would look like [tɹɒf].

- Word-final *-t* becomes *-r* when the next word begins with a vowel. Such words have often been written as single words dialect writing (*arrall* 'at all', *arrova* 'out of a', *birra* 'bit of', *burri* 'but I', *worrappenz* 'what happens', since this process is productive and applies before polysyllabic words as well, it has been written *-rr'* with the following word run-on here (*arr'all, ourr'of a, birr'o, burr'I, wharr'appens*).
- The *-t* to *-r* shift also sometimes happens within words (*gerrin* 'getting', *berrer* 'better') no apostrophe is used here as there is no word boundary. There is sometimes ambiguity vis à vis the standard language; compare *purrin* ['pʊɹɪn] 'putting' with *perrin* ['pɛɹɪn] 'purring'.

I would be interested to receive comment from readers regarding the suitability of this orthography for representing Scouse. Inevitably in such a venture there will be inconsistencies, of course. I trust these will not distract readers from their enjoyment of Marvin's splendid translation.

Michael Everson
Portlaoise, July 2015

Alice's Adventchers in Wunderland

Contints

Ollin de golden afternoon
  Dead leisurely we glide;
Both de paddles, wid little skill,
  By little arms are pulled,
While little ands pretends in vain
  Our wanderins to guide.

Ah, cruel Tree! In such an hour,
  Unner such dreamy weadder,
To beg a tale of breath too weak
  To ster de diddiest feadder!
Yet what can one poor gob avail
  Against tree tongues togedder?

Stuck-up Prima flashes fort
  Er order "to gerron it":
In gennler tones Secunda opes
  "Der'll be a lorra nonsense in it!"
While Tertia butts er ead in
  Not *more* dan once a minute.

An ay, to sudden silence won,
  In fancy dey persue
De dream-kid movin truw a land
  Of wunders wild an new,
In friendly chat wid berd or beast—
  An alf believe it true.

An ever, as de story drained
  De wells of fancy dry,
Dog-tired an weak and tired
  To sling irr'all on by,
"De rest next time—" "Irr'*is* next time!"
  De appy gobs all cry.

Dus grew de tale o Wunderland:
  Dus slowly, one by one,
Its quaint events were ammered out—
  An now de tale is done,
An ome we steer, a merry crew,
  Unner de settin sun.

Alice! A kiddies' story take,
  An wid a gentle and,
Stick it where Childhood's dreams are twined
  In Memry's mystic band,
Like pilgrim's widdered wreat o flowers
  Pluckd in a far-off land.

CHAPTER I

Down de Rabbit-Ole

Alice was gerrin dog-tired o sittin wid er sister on de bank, an avin nothin to do; once or twice she ad a butcher's at de buwk er sister was readin, burr'it ad no pitchures or werds in it, "an what's de use of a buwk," tought Alice, "widout pitchures an werds?"

So she was tinkin in er ead (as well as she could, for de ot day was makin er feel very sleepy an stupid), whedder i'was werth makin a daisy-chain, or was it werth de bodder o gerrin up to pick dem, when sunnly a white rabbit wid pink eyes ran close by er.

Der was nothin special in dat: nor did Alice tink it funny to ear de Rabbit say to itself, "Oh dear! Oh dear! I'm gonna be dead late!" When she tought abourr'it afterwerds, she reckoned she should ave could tought irr'a *bit* funny-like, burr'at de time irr'all seemed quite natchural); but when de Rabbit *took a watch ourr'of its waistcoat pockit*, an luwked arr'it, an urried on, she jumped up quick-like, for it flashed truw er ead dat she ad never eyeballed a Rabbit wid eider a waistcoat pockit or a ticker to take ourr'of it, an bein a bit nosy-like, she ran across de field after it, an was just in time to see it pop down a dirty great big Rabbit ole, unner de edge.

In a tick Alice was down after it, never once tinkin ow in de werld she was gonna gerr'out again.

De rabbit-ole went straight on like a tunnel for some way, an den dipped down sudden-like, so sudden dat Alice din't ave a minute to tink about stoppin erself before she found erself fallin down what seemed to be a very deep well.

Eider de well was very deep, or she was fallin dead slow, cause she ad plenny o time to gos around as she went down, an wunder what was gonna appen next. Ferst, she tried luwkin down to see what she was comin to, burr'it was like a coal-ole, too dark to see nothin: den she luwked at de sides o de well, an seen loads o cupboards an buwkshelves: ere an der she saw maps an pitchures ung on pegs. She gorr'a jar off of a shelf as she passed: i'was labelled "ORANGE MARMA-LADE", she was'n alf dissapointed cause der weren't nothin in it: she din't wanna drop de jar in case she done someone's ead in wid it, so she stuck irr'in a cupboard as she fell pass it.

"Well!" tought Alice to erself. "After fallin like dis, I wo'n wurry about fallin down our stairs again! Dey wo'n alf tink I'm ard when I get back to our ouse! I'would'n even bodder me if I fell off o de top of our ouse! An no kiddin eider!"

Down, down, down. Would de fall *never* come to an end? "I wunder ow many miles I've fallen by dis time?" She said aloud. "I muss be gerrin somewhere near de centre o de earth. Lemme see: dat would be four tousand miles down, I tink—" (For you see, Alice ad lernt some tings like dis at school, an dough it weren't a *very* good oppertchunity for bein big-eaded, as der was no-one to earwig it, still i'was good practice to say irr'over) "—Yeah, dat's about de right distance—burr'I wunder what Latitchude or Longitchude I've got to?" (Alice ad'n de foggiest what dey meant, like, but dey were custy big werds to say.)

Presently she began again. "I wunder if I'm gonna fall right *truw* de earth! Ow funny irr'll seem to come out among de people what wawk wid deir eads downwerds! De antipathies, I tink—" (she was made up no-one was earwiggin, dis time, as it din't sound arr'all de right werd) "—burr'I'll ave to ask dem wharr'it's called, you know. Ey, gerl, is dis dat New Zealand place? Or is it Ozzieland?" (An she tried to kertsey as she spoke—fancy *kertseyin* as you're fallin truw de air! D'you tink you could manidge it?) "An wharr'a higgorant little gerl she'll tink me for askin! Nah, irr'll never do to ask: peraps I'll see it written up some-where."

Down, down, down. Der was nothin else to do, so Alice soon began tawkin again. "Dinah'll miss me loads tonight, I'll betcha!" (Dinah was de moggy.) "I ope dey'll remember er dish o milk at tea-time. Dinah, me love! I wish you were down ere wid me, kiddo! Der ain't no mice in de air, I'm afraid, but you might catch a bat, an dey luwk just like a mouse, you know. But do moggies eat bats, I wunder?" An ere Alice was gerrin sleepy, an wenn on sayin to erself, in a dreamy sorr'o way, "Do moggies eat bats? Do moggies eat bats?" an sometimes, "Do bats eat moggies?" for, you see, as she could'n answer eider question, it din't marrer much which way she purr'it. She felt dat she was dozin off, an ad just begun to dream dat she was wawkin and in and wid Dinah, an was sayin to er dead serious-like, "Now Dinah, tell me de truth: did you ever scoff a bat?", when sunnly, tump! tump! down she came on a eap o sticks an dry leaves, an de fall was over.

Alice weren't a bit urt, an she jumped up on er feet in a tick: she luwked up, burr'it was all dark over-ead: before er was anudder long passidge, an de White Rabbit was still in sight, urryin down it. Der weren't a minute to lose: away went Alice like de wind, an was just in time to ear it say, as it went round de corner: "Oh me ears an whiskers, ow late it's gerrin!" She was close be'ind it when she terned de corner, but de Rabbit was no longer to be seen: she found erself in a long, low all, which was lit up by a row o lamps angin from de roof.

Der were doors all round de all, but dey was all locked; an when Alice ad been all de way down one side an up de udder tryin every door, she wawked sadly down de middle, wundrin ow she was ever gerrin out again.

Sunnly she saw a diddy little tree-legged table, all made o solid glass: der weren't nothin on it burr'a tiny golden key, an Alice's ferst idea was dis might belong to one o de doors o de all; but alas! eider de locks were too big, or de key too small, burr'at any rate i'would'n open none o dem. Owever, on de second time round, she come to a low kertain she ad seen before, an be'ind i'was a little door about fifteen inches igh: she tried de little golden key in de lock, an was made up when it fitted!

Alice opened de door an found dat it led into a small passidge, not much bigger dan a rat-ole: she knelt down an luwked along de passidge into de loveliest gardin you ever seen. Ow she longed to gerr'out o dat dark all, an wander about among de lovely flowerbeds an de cool fountains, but she could'n even gerr'er ead truw de doorway: "An even if me ead *would* go truw, "tought poor Alice, "I'would'n be any use widout me shoulders. Oh, ow I wish I could shurr'up like a telescope! I tink I could, if ony I knew ow to start." For, you see, so many out-o-de-way tings ad appened lately, dat Alice was beginnin to tink nothin was impossible.

Der weren't no use waitin by de little door, so she went back to de table, alf opin she might find anudder key on it, or at any rate a buwk o rules for shurrin up people like tele-scopes: dis time she found a little bottle on it ("Which certainly was'n ere before," said Alice), an tied round de neck o de bottle was a paper label, wid de werds "DRINK ME" written really lovely in big lerrers on it.

I'was all right sayin "Drink me", but wise little Alice was'n gonna fall for *dat* in a urry. "No, I'm gonna luwk ferst," she said, "an see whedder it says '*poison*' or not"; for she ad read loads o nice little stories about kids what ad got burnt, an eaten by wild animals, an udder orrible tings, all cause dey *would'n* remember de simple rules what deir mates ad tole dem, like, darr'a red-ot poker will burn you if you old it too long; an if you cuts your finger really deep wid a knife, it usually bleeds; an she ad never forgotten dat, if you drink much from a bottle marked "poison", irr'll allus bodder you, sooner or later.

Owever dis bottle *was'n* marked "poison", so Alice dared to taste it, an findin it dead nice (irr'ad, really, a sorr'o mixed flavour o cherry-tart, custid, pineapple, roast turkey, toffy, an ot buttered toast), she very soon finished irr'off.

"Wharr'a curious feelin!" said Alice. "I muss be shurrin up like a telescope!"

An so i'was indeed: she was now ony ten inches igh, an er face brightened up at de tought dat she was just de right size for goin truw de little door into dat lovely gardin. Ferst, owever, she ung on a tick to see if she was gonna shrink any ferder: she felt a little nervous about dis; "for it might end, you know," said Alice to erself, "in me goin out altogedder, like a candle. I wunder wharr'I should be like den?" An she tried to fancy what de flame of a candle luwks like after de candle is blown out, for she could'n remember ever avin seen such a ting.

After a while, findin dat nothin more was appenin, she decided on goin into de gardin at once; burr'alas for poor Alice! When she gorra de door, she found she ad forgot de little golden key, an when she went back to de table for it, she found der was no way to reach it: she could see it quite plainly truw de glass an she tried er best to climb up one o de legs o de table, burr'it was too slippery; an when she ad worn erself out wid tryin, de poor little ting sat down an cried.

"Come, der's no use in cryin like dat!" said Alice to erself, radder sharply. "I advise you to leave off dis minute!" She genrally gave erself very good advice (dough she din't offen follie it), an sometimes she tole erself off so ard to bring tears to er eyes; an once she remembered tryin to box er own ears for avin cheated erself in a game o crokay she was playin against erself, for dis curious kid was dead fond o pretendin to be two people. "Burr'it's no use now," tought poor Alice, "to pretend to be two people! Why, der's ardly enough o me left to make one proper person!"

Soon er eyes fell on a little glass box dat was lyin unner de table: she opened it, an found in it a very small cake, irr'ad "EAT ME" on it, done dead lovely in currints. "Well I'll eat it, "said Alice, "an if it makes me grow larger, I can reach de key; an if it makes me grow smaller, I can creep unner de door: so eider way I'll gerr'into de gardin, an I do'n care wharr'appens!"

She ate a little bit, an said anxiously to erself, "Which way? Which way?", oldin er and on de top of er bonce to feel which way it were growin; an she was quite suprised to find dat she remained de same size. Te be sure, dis is what genrally appens when one eats cake; burr'Alice ad got so much in de way of expectin nothin burr'out-o-de-way tings to appen, darr'it seemed quite dull an stupid for life to go on in de common way.

So she set to werk, an very soon finished off de cake.

CHAPTER II

De Pool o Tears

"Curiouser an curiouser!" cried Alice (she was so much gobsmacked, dat for de momint she quite forgot ow to speak good English). "Now I'm openin out like de largest telescope darr'ever was! Good-bye, feet!" (for when she gozzed down arr'er feet, dey seemed to be miles away, dey were gerrin so far off). "Oh, me poor little feet, I wunder oo'll purr'on your shoes an stockins for you now, dears? I'm sure *I* shan't be able! I shall be a great deal too far off to bodder meself about you: you muss manidge de best way you can—burr'I muss be kind to dem," tought Alice, "or peraps dey wo'n wawk de way I wanna go! Lemme see. I'll give dem a new pair o boots every Chrissmas."

An she wenn on plannin to erself ow she would manidge it. "Dey muss go by de carrier," she tought; "an ow funny irr'll seem, sendin prezzies to your own feet! An ow odd de directions'll luwk!

Alice's Right Foot, Esq.
    Arthrug,
        near de Fender,
          (wid Alice's love).
Oh dear, wharr'a load o rubbish I'm tawkin!"

Just at dis momint er ead struck against de roof o de all: in fack she was now radder more dan nine feet igh, an all at once she grabbed de little golden key an scarpered off to de gardin door.

Poor Alice! I'was as much as she could do, lyin down on one side, to luwk truw into de gardin wid one eye; but to get truw der weren't no chance wharr'ever: she sat down an terned on de waterworks.

"You oughta be ashamed o yourself," said Alice, "A derty great big gerl like you" (she might well say dis), "Te go on cryin in dis way! Stop dis minute, I tell you!" But she wenn on all de same, sheddin buckits o tears, until der was a large pool all around er, an four inches deep an reachin alf down de all.

After a time she eard a little pattrin o feet in de distance, an she astily dried er eyes to see what was comin. It were de White Rabbit comin back, dressed to de nines, wid a pair o white kid-gloves in one and an a large fan in de udder: e came trottin along in a great urry, muttrin to izself as e came, "Oh! De Duchess, de Duchess! Oh! She wo'n *alf* be mad if I've kept er angin round!" Alice was so desprate dat she was ready to ask elp from anybody: so, when de Rabbit came near er, she began, in a low, timid voice, "If you please, ser—" De Rabbit near jumped ourr'of iz skin, dropped de white kid-gloves an de fan, an scurried away into de darkness as ard as e could go.

Alice took up de fan an gloves, an, as de all was dead ot, she kept fannin erself all de time she wenn on tawkin. "Dear, dear! Ow queer everytin is today! An ony yisterdy tings wenn on just as usual. I wunder if I've been changed in de night? Lemme tink: *was* I de same when I gorr'up dis mornin? I almost tink I can remember feelin a bit diffrent. Burr'if I'm not de same, de next question is, 'Oo in de werld am I?' Ah, *dat's* de great puzzle!" An she began tinkin over all de kids she knew dat were all de same age as erself, to see if she could ave been changed for any o dem.

"I'm sure I'm not Ada," she said, "For er air goes in such long ringlits, an mine do'n go in ringlits arr'all; an I'm sure I ain't Mabel, for I know loads o tings, an she do'n know nothin! Besides, *she's* she, an *I'm* me, an—oh dear, ow puzzlin irr'all is! I'll see if I know all de tings I used to. Lemme see: four times five is twelve, an four times six is terteen, an four times seven is—oh dear! I'll never get to twenny at dis rate! Owever, de sums table do'n signify: lets try Geography. London is de capital o Paris, an Paris is de capital o Rome, an Rome—no, *dat's* all wrong, I'm sure! I must ave been changed for Mabel! I'll try an say *'Ow doth de little—'*," an she crossed er ands on er lap as if she were sayin lessins, an began to repeat it, burr'er voice sounded oarse an strange, an de werds din't come de same as de should've:—

> *"Ow doth de little crocodile*
> *Improve iz shinin tale,*
> *An pour de waters o de Nile*
> *On every golden scale!*
>
> *"Ow cheerfully e seems to grin,*
> *An neatly spreads iz claws,*
> *An welcomes little fishes in,*
> *Wid gently smilin jaws!"*

"I'm sure dose aren't de right werds," said poor Alice, an er eyes filled wid tears again as she wenn on. "I muss be Mabel, after all, an I'll ave to go an live in dat poky little ouse, an ave next to no toys to play wid, an oh, loads o lessins to lern! No, I've made up me mind about it: if I'm Mabel, I'll stay down ere! Irr'll be no use deir purr'in deir eads down an sayin 'Come up again, dear!' I shall ony luwk up an say 'Oo am I, den? Tell me dat ferst, an den, if I like dat person, I'll come up: if not, I'll stay down ere till I'm somebody else'— but, oh dear!" cried Alice, wid a sudden burst o tears, "I do wish dey *would* put deir eads down! I'm fed up o bein all alone ere!"

As she said dis she luwked down arr'er ands, an was suprised to see dat she'd purr'on one o de Rabbit's little white kid-gloves while she was tawkin. "Ow *can* I ave done dat?" she tought. "I muss be growin small again." She gorr'up an went to de table to measure erself by it, an found dat, as near as she could guess, she was now about two feet igh, an was goin on shrinkin dead quick: she soon found out dat de cause o dis was de fan she was oldin, an slung it quick-like, just in time to save erself from shrinkin away to nothin.

"Dat was'n *alf* a close shave!" said Alice, she bottled one good stile at de sudden change, but weren't alf made up to find erself still alive. "An now for de gardin!" An she run like de clappers back to de little door; burr'ard luck! de little door was shurr'again, an de little golden key was lyin on de table like de lass time, "tings as gone from bad to werse," tought de poor kid, "for I weren't never as titchy as dis before, never! An I say darr'it's too bad, darr'it is!"

As she spoke dese werds er foot slipped, an in a tick, splash! she was up to er neck in sea water. Er ferst tought was dat she'd some-ow fell in de sea, "an in dat case I can go back by train," she said to erself. (Alice ad been to de seaside once in er life, an ad come to de genral conclusion, dat no marrer where you go on de English coast you find a lorr'o bathin machines in de sea, some kids diggin in de sand wid wooden spades, den a row o doss-ouses, an be'ind dem a railway station.) Owever she soon made out dat she was in de pool o tears which she ad wept when she was nine feet igh.

"I wish I ad'n ave cried so much!" said Alice, as she swum about, tryin to find er way out. "I should gerr'it in de neck for it now, I reckon, by bein drownded in me own tears! Darr'll be a strange ting, an no messin! Anyway, everytin is strange today."

Just den she eard sometin splashin around in de pool a little way off, an she swum nearer to take a dekko: at ferst she tought darr'it muss be a walrus or ippopotamus, but den she remembered ow small she was now, an she soon made out darr'i'was ony a mouse darr'ad fell in like she ad.

"Would it be wert it," tought Alice, "to speak to dis mouse? Every ting is so out-o-de-way down ere, darr'I bet it can tawk: arr'any rate, der's no arm in askin." So she began: "O Mouse, d'you know de way ourr'o dis pool? I am gerrin cheesed off o swimmin about ere, O Mouse!" (Alice tought dis muss be de right way o tawkin to a mouse: she ad'n never done such a ting before, but she remembered avin seen in er brudder's Latin Grammar, "A mouse—of a mouse—to a mouse—a mouse—O mouse!) De mouse luwked arr'er funny-like, an seemed to er to wink wid one of its little eyes, burr'it said nothin.

"Peraps it do'n unnerstand English," tought Alice. "I daresay it's a French mouse, come over wid William de Conqueror." (For, wid all er knowlidge of istry, Alice din't ave a clue ow long ago anytin ad appened.) So she began again: "Où est ma chatte?" which was de ferst sentince in er French lessin buwk. De Mouse gave a sudden leap ourr'o de water, an seemed to quiver all over wid fright. "Oh, beggin your pardon!" cried Alice, scared dat she mighrr'ave urt de poor animal's feelins. "I quite forgot you din't care much for moggies."

"Not like moggies!" cried de Mouse, in a shrill, passionate voice. "Would *you* like moggies, if you were me?"

"Well peraps not," said Alice in a soothin tone: "Do'n get sherty-like wid me abourr'it. An yerr'I wish you could see our moggy Dinah. I tink you'd take a shine to moggies if you could see er. She's such a lovely quiet ting!" Alice wenn on alf to erself, as she swum: lazily about in de pool, "an she sits purr'in so nicely by de fire, lickin er paws an washin er face—an she's such a nice soff ting to cuddle—an she's boss for catchin mice—oh, I'm sorry, mush!" cried Alice again, for dis time de Mouse was brisslin all over, an she was sure i'was really offended. "We wo'n tawk about er anymore if you do'n wanna."

"We, indeed!" cried de Mouse, oo was tremblin down to de end of its tale. "As if *I* would tawk about such a ting! Our lot's allus *ated* moggies: nasty, low, common tings! Do'n let me ear de name again!"

"I wo'n indeed!" said Alice, in a great urry to change de subject o conversation. "Are you—are you fond—o—o dogs?" De Mouse din't answer, so Alice wenn on eagerly:

der's a nice little dog near our ouse I'd like to show you! A little bright-eyed terrier, you know, wid oh, such long kerly brown air! An irr'll fetch tings when you trow dem, an irr'll sit up an beg for its dinner, an all sorts o tings—I caan't remember alf o dem—an it belongs to a farmer, you know, an e says it kills all de rats an—oh dear!" cried Alice in a sorraful tone, "I'm afraid I've offended irr'again!" For de Mouse was swimmin away from er as ard as it could go, an makin a load o noise in de pool as it went.

So she called soffly after it. "Mouse, dear! Do come back again, an we wo'n tawk about moggies or dogs eider, if you do'n like dem!" When de Mouse eard dis, it terned round and swum slowly back to er: its face was quite pale (wid passion, Alice tought), an it said in a low tremblin voice, "Lerr'us get to de shore, an den I'll tell you me istry, an you'll unnerstand why irr'is I caan't stand moggies an dogs."

I'was igh time to skedaddle, for de pool was gerrin quite chocka wid de berds an animals darr'ad fell in it: der was a Duck an a Dodo, a Lory, an a Eaglet, an loads of udder curious creatchers. Alice led de way, an dey all swum to de shore

CHAPTER III

A Caucus-Race
an a Long Tale

Dey were not alf a queer luwkin lot dat gaddered on de bank—de berds wid scraggy feadders, de animals wid deir fur clingin close to dem, an all drippin wet, cross, en feelin ourr'o place.

De ferst ting was, o course, ow ta gerr'em dry again: dey ad a conflab abourr'it, an after a couple o minutes it seemed quite natchural to Alice to find erself tawkin dead pally wid dem, as if she'd known dem all er life. Indeed, she ad quite a long argument wid de Lory, oo at last gorr'a right gob on it, an would ony say "I am older dan you, an muss know berrer." Alice was avin none of it widout knowin ow old i'was, an, as de Lory would'n lerr'on ow old i'was, der was no more to be said.

At last de Mouse, oo seemed to be de ead bottlewasher o dis lot, called out "Sit down, you lot, an lissen to me! *I'll* soon make you dry enough!" Dey all sat down sharpish-like in a large ring, wid de Mouse in de miggle. Alice kept er eyes anxiously fixed on it, for she felt sure she would'n alf catch a bad cold if she din't get dry dead soon.

"Ahem!" said de Mouse wid an importint air. "Are youse all ready? Dis is de driest ting I know. Keep stumm-like, okay! 'William de Conqueror, oose course was a winner wid de pope, soon got de berrer o de English, oo wanted leaders, an dey ad got used to bein trampled on. Edwin an Morcar, de earls o Mercia an Nortumbria—'"

"Ugh!" said Lory, wid a shiver.

"Ya, what!" said de Mouse, frownin, but dead polite. "Did you speak?"

"Norr'I!" said de Lory astily.

"I tought you did," said de Mouse. "I carry on. 'Edwin an Morcar, de earls o Mercia an Nortumbria, were on iz side; an even Stigand, de patriotic archbishop o Canterbury, found it advisable—'"

"Found *what*?" said de Duck.

"Found *it*," de Mouse replied radder crossly: "o course you know what 'it' means."

"I know what 'it' means all right, when I find a ting," said de Duck: "it's genrally a frog or a werm. De ting is, what did de archbishop find?"

De Mouse din't notice dis question, but urriedly wenn on, "'—found it advisable to go wid Edgar Atheling to meet William an offer im de crown. William acted all right at ferst. But de cheek of iz Normans—' Ow you doin now, love?" it when on, ternin to Alice as it spoke.

"As wet as ever," said Alice in a melancholy tone: "it do'n seem to dry me arr'all."

"In dat case," said de Dodo solemnly, risin to its feet, "Stow dis lot, eh, an go on to sometin more berrer—"

"Speak more proper!" said de Eaglet. "I do'n know alf what you're on about, an I do'n tink you do neider!" An de Eaglet bent down its ead to ide a smile: ya could ear some o de udder berds titterin loud-like.

"Wharr'I was gonna say," said de Dodo in a offended tone, "was, dat de best ting to gerr'us dry would be a caucus-race."

"Wharr'is a Caucus-race when its arr'ome?" said Alice; not dat she was boddered anyway, but de Dodo ad paused as if it tought dat *somebody* oughta speak, an nobody seemed to be boddered arr'all.

"Why," said de Dodo, "de best way to explain irr'is to do it." (An as you might like to try it yourself some winter day, I'll tell you ow de Dodo manidged it.)

Ferst it marked out a race-course, in a sorr'o circle ("de exack shape do'n marrer," it said), an den de lorr'o dem were purr'along de course, ere an der. Der was no "One, two, tree, an away," but dey began runnin when dey liked, an left off when dey liked, so darr'i'was'n easy to know when de race was over. Owever, when dey'd been runnin alf an hour or so, an were quite dry again, de Dodo sunnly called out "De race is over!" an dey all crowded round it, pantin, an askin "But oo's won?"

Dis question de Dodo could'n answer widout a lorr'o tought, an it stud for a long time wid one finger pressed on its fore-ead (de way you used to see Shakespeare, in iz pitchures, like), while de rest waited in silence. At last de Dodo said "*Everyone* as won, an *all* must ave prizes."

"Burr'oo is to give de prizes?" quite a lorr'o dem asked.

"Why, *she*, o course," said de Dodo, pointin arr'Alice wid one finger, an de ole lorr'o dem all crowded round er, callin out in a confused way, "Prizes! Prizes!"

Alice din't ave de foggiest what to do, an in dispair she purr'er and in er pockit, an pulled ourr'a box o comfits (luckly de salt water ad'n gorr'in it), an anded dem round as prizes. Dey all gorr'exackly one each.

"But she must ave a prize erself, you know," said de Mouse.

"Of course," de Dodo replied dead serious-like.

"Wharr'else ave you gorr'in your pockit?" it wenn on, ternin to Alice. "Ony a timble," said Alice sadly.

"And irr'over ere," said de Dodo.

Den dey all crowded round er onee more, while de Dodo solemnly gave er de timble, sayin, "We beg your acceptince o dis elegant timble"; an, when irr'ad finished dis short speech, dey all cheered.

Alice tought de ole ting dead daft, but dey all luwked so serious she din't dare to laugh; an, as she could'n tink what to say, she just bowed, an took de timble, luwkin as solemn as she could.

De next ting was to eat de comfits: dis caused some noise an confusion, as de large berds complained de could'n taste deirs, an de small ones choked an ad to be patted on de back. Owever, i'was over at last, an de sat down again in a ring, an begged de Mouse to tell dem sometin more.

"You promised to tell me your istry, you know," said Alice, "an why irr'is you ate—M an D," she added in a whisper, alf afraid darr'i'would get de ump again.

"Mine is a long·an sad tale!" said de Mouse ternin to Alice, an sighin.

"Irr'is a long tail certainly," said Alice, luwkin down wid wunder at de Mouse's tail; "but why do you call it sad, eh?" An she kept on puzzlin about it while de Mouse was speakin, so darr'er idea o de tale was sometin like dis:—

"Fury said to
a mouse, Dat
e met in de
ouse, 'Lerr'us
both go
to law: *I*
will prose-
cute *you*.—
Come, I'll
take no de-
nial: We
must ave
de trial;
For really
dis morn-
in I've
nothin
to do.'
Said de
mouse to
de cur,
'Such a
trial, dear
ser, Wid
no jury
or judge,
would
be wast-
in our
breath.'
'I'll be
judge,
I'll be
jury,'
said
cun-
nin
ould
Fury:
'I'll
try
de
ole
cause,
an
con-
demn
you
to
death.'

"You're not attendin!" said de Mouse to Alice severely. "Wharr'are you tinkin of?"

28

"Sorry der, lar," said Alice dead umble-like; "you'd gorra de fifth bend, I tink?"

"I ad *not!*" cried de Mouse, sharply an dead cobby-like.

"A knot!" said Alice, allus ready to make erself useful, an luwkin anxiously about er. "Oh, do let me elp to undo it!"

"I shall do nothin o de sort," said de Mouse, gerrin up an wawkin away. "You show me up by tawkin such a load o tripe!"

"I din't mean it!" pleaded poor Alice. "But you so easily lose your rag you know!"

De Mouse ony growled in reply.

"Please come back an finish your story!" Alice called after it. An all de udders joined in togedder. "Yeah, go ead, eh!" But de Mouse ony shook its ead impatiently an wawked a little quicker.

"Wharr'a pity i'would'n stay!" sighed de Lory; as soon as i'was quite ourr'o sight. An an ould Crab took de oppertchunity o sayin to er daughter, "Ah, me gerl! Lerr'it be a lessin to you never to lose *your* temper!"

"Old your tongue, Ma!" said de young Crab, a little snappishly. "You're enough to try de patience of an oyster!"

"I wish I ad our Dinah ere, I know I do!" said Alice aloud, addressin no one in particular. "*She'd* soon fetch it back!"

"An oo is Dinah, when she's arr'ome-like, eh?" said de Lory.

Alice replied eagerly, for she was allus more dan ready to tawk abourr'er pet: "Dinah's our moggy, an she's such a great one for catchin mice, an no kiddin! An oh, I wish you could see er after de berds! Why, she'll eat a little berd as soon as luwk arr'it!"

De speech caused a right ster among de lorr'o dem. Some o de berds took off at once: one ould Magpie began rappin itself up dead careful, sayin "I really muss be gerrin ome: de night air do'n suit me troat!" an a Canary called out in a tremblin voice to its kids "Come ead, me loves! Its igh time you were all up de dancers an conko!" On various pretexts dey all moved off, an Alice was left on er todd.

"I wish I ad'n'a mentioned Dinah!" she said to erself in a melancholy tone. "Nobody seems to like er, down ere, an I'm sure she's de best moggy in de werld! Oh, me lovely Dinah! I wunder if I'll ever see you any more!" An ere poor Alice began to cry again, for she felt dead lonely an down in de dumps. In a little while, owever, she again eard a pattrin o little footsteps in de distince, an she luwked up eagerly, alf opin dat de Mouse ad changed iz mind, an was comin back to finish iz story.

CHAPTER IV

De Rabbit Sends in a Little Bill

T'was de White Rabbit, trottin slowly back again, an luwkin anxiously about as it went, as if irr'ad lost sometin; an she eard it muttrin to itself, "De Duchess! De Duchess! Oh me dear paws! Oh me fur an whiskers! She'll get me exeecuted, as sure as ferrits is ferrits! Where *can* I ave dropped dem, I wunder?" Alice guessed in a momint darr'i'was luwkin for de fan an de pair o white kid-gloves, an she very good-natchuredly began untin about for dem, but dey were nowhere to be seen—every ting seemed to ave changed since er swim in de pool, an de great all, wid de glass table an de little door, ad vanished completely.

Very soon de Rabbit noticed Alice, as she wenn untin about, an called out to er in n angry tone, "Why, Mary Ann, wharr'*are* you doin out ere? Run ome at once, an fetch me a per o gloves an a fan! Quick, now," an Alice was so scared dat she ran off at once in de direction it pointed to, widout tryin to explain de mistake irr'ad made.

"E took me for iz ousemade," she said to erself as she ran. "Ow suprised e'll be when e finds out oo I am! Burr'I'd bedder take im iz fan an gloves—darr'is, if I can find em." As she said dis she came upon a neat little ouse, on de door irr'ad a bright brass plate wid de name "W. RABBIT" engraved upon it. She wenn in widout knockin, an urried up stairs, panickin in case she'd meet de real Mary Ann, an be terned ourr'o de ouse before she'd found de fan an gloves.

"Ow queer it seems, " Alice said to erself, "to be goin messidges for a rabbit! I suppose Dinah'll be sendin me on messidges next!" An she began fancyin de sorr'o ting dat would appen: "'Miss Alice! Come ead, an get ready for your wawk!' 'Comin in a minute, nerse! Burr'I've gorra watch dis mouse-ole till Dinah comes back, an see dat de mouse do'n gerr'out.' Ony I do'n tink," Alice when on, "dat dey'd let Dinah stop in de ouse if she began ordrin people about like dat!"

By dis time she'd found er way into a tidy little room, wid a table in de winda, an on it (as she'd oped) a fan an two or tree pairs o tiny white kid-gloves: she took up de fan an a pair o de gloves, an was just gonna leave de room, when er eyes fell on a little bottle dat stud near de luwkin-glass. Der was'n no label dis time wid de werds "DRINK ME", but all de same she uncorked it an purr'it to er lips. "I know *sometin* intrestin is sure to appen," she said to erself, "Whenever I eat or drink anytin: so I'll just see what dis bottle does. I do ope irr'll make me grow large again, for I'm really sick o bein such a diddy little ting!"

It did so indeed, an much sooner dan she'd expected: before she'd drunk alf de bottle she found er ead pressin against de ceilin, an ad to stoop to save er neck from bein broken. She astily purr'it down, sayin "Darr'll do—I ope I wo'n grow anymore—I caan't gerr'out de door as it is—I wish I ad'n'a drunk such a lorr'of it!"

Alas! I'was to late to wish dat! She wenn on growin, an growin, an very soon ad to kneel down on de floor: in anudder minute der was norr'even room for dis, an she tried de effect o lyin down wid one elba against de door, an de udder arm kerled round er ead. Still she wenn on growin, an, as a last resource, she put one arm ourr'o de winda, an one foot up de chimbley, an said to erself, "Now I can do no more, no madder wharr'appens. Wharr'ever'll become o me?"

Luckly for Alice, de little magic bottle ad now ad its full effect, an she din't grow no more: still i'was dead uncomfy, an as der din't seem no chance of er ever gerrin ourr'o de room again, no wunder she felt dead un-appy.

"I'was much berrer at ome," tought poor Alice, "when you weren't always growin bigger an smaller, an bein ordered about by mice an rabbits. I almost wish I ad'n'a gone down dat rabbit-ole—an yet—an yet—it's curious, you know, dis sorr'o life! I wunder what can ave appened to me! When I used to read fairy-tales, I fancied dat kind o ting never appened, an now ere I am in de miggle o one. Der oughta be a buwk writ about me, I'm not kiddin neider! An when I grow up, I'll write one—burr'I'm grown up now," she added in a dead sad voice: "arr'any rate der ain't no room to grow up anymore in *ere*."

"But den," tought Alice, "shall I *never* gerr'any oulder dan I am now? Darr'll be a comfort, one way—never to be a ould woman—but den—allus to ave lessins to lern! Oh, I would'n like *dat*!"

"Oh, you foolish Alice!" she answered erself. "Ow can you lern lessins in ere? Why, der's ardly room for *you*, lerr'alone any lessin buwks!"

An so she when on, takin ferst one side an den de udder. An makin a right conflab ourr'of it an no messin; burr'after a few minutes she eard a voice outside, an stopped to earwig it.

"Mary Ann! Mary Ann!" said de voice. "Fetch me me gloves dis minute!" Den came a pattrin o little feet on de stairs. Alice knew i'was de Rabbit comin to luwk for er, an she trembled till she shook de ouse, quite forgettin dat she was abourr'a tousand times bigger dan de Rabbit, an ad no reason to be scared of it.

Presently de Rabbit came up to de door, an tried to open it; burr'as de door opened inwerds, an Alice's elba was pressed ard against it, nothin appened. Alice eard it say to itself "Den I'll go round an gerr'in at de winda."

"You wo'n, you know, lar!" tought Alice, an, after waitin till she fancied she eard de Rabbit just unner de winda, she sunnly spread ourr'er and, an made a snatch in de air. She din't gerr'old o nothin, but she eard a little shriek an a fall, an a crash o broken glass, from which she concluded darr'i'was just possible irr'ad fell in a cucumber-frame, or sometin like dat.

Next came a narky voice—de Rabbit's—"Pat! Pat! Where are you?" An den a voice she ad'n eard before, "Sure then I'm here! Digging for apples, yer honour!"

"Diggin for apples, indeed!" said de Rabbit dead narky. "Ere! Come an elp me ourr'o *dis*!" (Sounds o more broken glass.) "Now tell me, Pat, what's in dat winda?"

"Sure, it's an arm, yer honour!" (E said it like "arrum".)

"An arm, you goose! Ooever saw one dat size? Why, it fills de ole winda!"

"Sure it does, yer honour: but it's an arm for all that."

"Well irr'ain't got no business der, arr'any rate: go an get shut of it!"

Der was a long silence after dis, an Alice could ony ear whispers now an den, such as, "Sure, I don't like it, yer honour, at all, at all!" "Do as I tell you, you coward!" an at last she spread ourr'er and again, an made anudder snatch in de air. Dis time der were *two* little shrieks, an more sounds o broken glass. "Wharr'a load o cucumber-frames der muss be!" tought Alice."I wunder what dey'll do next! As for pullin me ourr'o de winda, I ony wish dey *could*! I'm sure *I* do'n wanna stay in ere no longer!"

She waited for some time widout earin nothin more: at last came a rumblin o little cart-wheels, an de sound of a load o voices all gabblin on togedder: she made out de werds: "Where's de udder ladder?—Why, I'd ony to bring de one. Bill's got de udder one—Bill! Gerr'it over ere, lad!—Ere, purr'em up at dis corner—No, tie dem togedder ferst—dey do'n reach alf igh enough yet—Oh! dey'll do about right. Do'n be particular—Ere Bill! Catch a-old o dis rope—Will de roof bear?—Mind dat loose slate—Oh, it's comin down! Eads below!" (a loud crash)—"Now oo did dat?—I'was Bill, I fancy—Oo's to go down de chimbley?—Naw, *I* ain't! *You* do it!—*Darr'*I wo'n, den!—Bill's gorra go down—Ere, Bill! De master says you've gorra go down de chimbley!"

"Oh! So Bill's gorra come down de chimbley, as e?" said Alice to erself. "Why, dey seem to purr'every ting on Bill! I would'n be in Bill's place for anytin: dis fireplace is too narra, an no kiddin; burr'I *tink* I can kick a little bit!"

She drew er foot as far down de chimbley as she could, an waited till she eard a little animal (she could'n guess what sorr'i'was) scratchin an scramblin about in de chimbley close a-by er: den sayin to erself "Dis is Bill," she gave one sharp kick, an waited to see what would appen next.

De ferst ting she eard was a genral chorus o "Der goes Bill!" den de Rabbit's silence, an den anudder confusion o voices—"Old up iz ead—Brandy now—Do'n choke im—Ow was it, ould feller? Wharr'appened to you? Tell us all abourr'it!"

At last came a feeble, squeakin voice (Dat's Bill," tought Alice), "Well, I ardly know—No more, tank you; I'm berrer now—burr'I'm a bit too flustered to tell you— all I know is, sometin comes at me like a Jack-in-de-box, an up I goes like a sky-rockit!"

"So you, did ould feller!" said de udders.

"We gorra burn de ouse down!" said de Rabbit's voice. An Alice called out as loud as she could, "If you do I'll set Dinah on to you!"

Der was a dead silence instintly, an Alice tought to erself "I wunder what dey'll do next! If dey ad any sense, dey'd take de roof off." After a minute or two dey began movin about again, an Alice eard de Rabbit say, "A barraful will do, to begin wid."

"A barraful o *what?*" tought Alice. But she din't ave long to doubt, for de next minute a shower o little pebbles came rattlin in at de winda, an some o dem itt er in de gob. "I'll purr'a stop to dis," she said to erself, an shouted out, "You'd berrer not do dat again or else!" which made it go dead quiet again.

Alice noticed wid some suprise dat de pebbles were all ternin inte little cakes as de lay on de floor, an a bright idea came into er ead. "If I eat one o dese cakes," she tought, "it's sure to make *some* change in me size; an, as it caan't possibly make me bigger, it muss make me smaller, I suppose."

So she swallied one o de cakes, an was made up to find dat she began shrinkin der an den. As soon as she was small enough to get truw de door, she ran ourr'o de ouse, an found quite a lorr'o little animals an berds waitin outside. De poor little Lizard, Bill, was in de miggle, bein eld up by two guinea-pigs, oo were givin it sometin ourr'of a bottle. Dey all made a rush arr'Alice de minute she appeared; but she give it toes as ard as she could, an soon found erself safe in a tick wood.

"De ferst ting I gorra do," said Alice to erself, as she wandered about in de wood, "is to grow to me right size again an de second ting is to find me way inte dat lovely gardin. I tink darr'll be de best plan."

It sounded an excellent plan, too right, an dead neat an simply arranged; de ony drawback was, she din't ave a clue ow to set about it; an, while she was eyeballin round anxiously among de trees, a little sharp bark just over er ead made er luwk up in a great urry.

A ginormous puppy was luwkin down arr'er wid big round eyes, an feebly stretchin out one paw, tryin to touch er. "Poor little ting!" said Alice, in a coaxin tone, an she tried ard to whistle to it; but she was really scared all de time at de tought darr'it might be ungry, in which case i'would very likely gobble er up in spite of all er coaxin.

Ardly knowin what she did, she picked up a little birr'o stick, an eld irr'out to de puppy: whereupon de puppy jumped in de air off all its feet at once, wid a yelp o delight, an rushed at de stick, an pretended to wurry it: den Alice dodged be'ind a great tissle, to keep erself from bein run over; an de momint she appeared on de udder side, de puppy made anudder rush at de stick, an tumbled ead over eels in its urry to gerr'old of it: den Alice, tinkin i'was just like playin a game wid a cart-orse, an expectin all de time to be trampled unner its feet, ran round de tissle again: den de puppy began a series o short charges at de stick, runnin a little bit more forwerds each time an a long way back, an barkin oarsely all de while, till at last it sat down a good way off, pantin, wid its tongue angin ourr'of its mout, an its big eyes alf shut.

Dis seemed to Alice de best time to do a bunk: so she set off at once, an ran till she was dead knackered, an till she could ardly ear de puppy bark.

"An yet wharr'a lovely puppy it were an all!" said Alice, as she leaned on a buttercup to rest erself, an fanned erself wid one o de leaves, "I should've liked lernin it tricks really much, if—if I'd ony been de right size to do it, like! Oh dear! I'd nearly forgot darr'I've gorra grow up again! Lemme see—ow is it to be manidged? I suppose I oughta eat or drink sometin or udder; but de great question is, 'What?'"

De great question certainly was, "What?" Alice ad a quick gander all round er at de flowers an de blades o grass, but she could'n see nothin dat luwked de right ting to eat or drink unner de circumstances. Der was a large mushroom growin near er, about as big as erself, an when she'd luwked unner it, an on both sides of it, an be'ind it, irr'occurred to er dat she mighrr'as well luwk an see what was on de top of it.

She stretched erself up on tiptoe, an peeped over de edge o de mushroom, an er eyes immediately met dose of a large blue caterpilla, dat was sittin on de top wid its arms folded, quietly smokin a long ookah, an takin not de smallest notice of er or of anytin else.

CHAPTER V

Advice from a Caterpilla

*D*e Caterpilla an Alice luwked arr'each udder for some time in silence: at last de Caterpilla took de ookah ourr'of its mout, an addressed er in a languid, sleepy voice.

"Oo are *you*?" said de Caterpilla.

Dis was norr'an encouridgin openin for a conversation. Alice replied, radder shy-like, "I—I ardly know, Ser, just at present—at least I know oo I *was* when I gorr'up dis mornin, burr'I tink I must ave been changed sevral times since den."

"What do you mean by dat?" said de Caterpilla sternly. "Explain yourself!"

"I caan't explain *meself*, I'm afraid, Ser," said Alice, "because I'm not meself, you see."

"I do'n see," said de Caterpilla.

"I'm afraid I caan't purr'it more clearly," Alice replied dead politely, "for I caan't unnerstand it meself to begin wid; an bein so many diffrent sizes in a day is dead confusin."

"Irr'is'n," said de Caterpilla.

41

"Well peraps you ain't found it so yet," said Alice, "but when you've to tern into a chrysalis—you will some day, you know—an den after dat into a butterfly, I should tink you'll feel irr'a little queer, wo'n you?"

"Norr'a bit," said de Caterpilla.

"Well peraps *your* feelins may be diffrent," said Alice: "all I know is i'would feel very queer to *me*."

"You!" said de Caterpilla contemptuously. "Oo are *you*?"

Which brought dem back again to de beginnin o de conversation. Alice felt a little irritated at de Caterpilla's makin such *dead* short remarks, an she drew erself up an said, dead serious, "I tink you oughta tell me oo you are, ferst."

"Why?" said de Caterpilla.

Ere was anudder puzzlin question; an, as Alice could'n tink of any good reason, an de Caterpilla seemed to ave a right cob on, she terned away.

"Come back!" de Caterpilla called after er. "I've sometin importint to say!" Dis sounded promisin, certainly. Alice terned an went back again.

"Keep your temper," said de Caterpilla.

"Is dat all?" said Alice, swallyin down er anger as well as she could.

"No," said de Caterpilla.

Alice tought she mighrr'as well wait, as she ad nothin else to do, an peraps after all it might tell er sometin wert earin. For some minutes it puffed away widout speakin; burr'at last irr'unfolded its arms, took de ookah ourr'of its mout again, an said "So you tink you're changed, do you?"

"I'm afraid I am, Ser," said Alice, "I caan't remember tings like I used to—an I do'n keep de same size for ten minutes togedder!"

"Caa'n't remember *what* tings?" said de Caterpilla.

"Well I've tried to say '*Ow doth de little busy bee*', burr'it all came out diffrent!" Alice replied in a very melancholy voice.

"Repeat '*You're ould, Faader William*'," said de Caterpilla.

Alice folded er ands, an began:—

"You're ould, Faader William," de young man said,
"An your air as become very white;
An yet you incessantly stand on your ead—
Do you tink, at your age, irr'is right?"

"In me youth," Farder William replied to iz son,
"I feared it might injure de brain;
But, now dat I'm perfeckly sure I ave none,
Why, I do it again an again."

"You're ould," said de youth, "as I mentioned before,
  An ave grown most uncommonly fat;
Yet you terned a back-somersault in at de door—
  Pray, wharr'is de reason o dat?"

"In me youth," said de sage, as e shook iz grey locks,
  "I kept all me limbs dead supple
By de use o dis ointmint—one shillin a box—
  Allow me to sell you a couple?"

"You're ould," said de youth, "an your jaws is to weak
    For anytin tougher dan suet;
Yet you finished de goose, wid de bones an de beak—
    Pray ow did you manidge to do it?"

"In me youth," said iz dad, "I took to de law
    An argued each case wid me wife;
An de muscular strenff, which it gave to me jaw,
    As lasted de rest o me life."

"You're ould," said de youth, "one would ardly suppose
  Dat your eye were as steady as ever;
Yet you balanced an eel on de end o your nose—
  What made you so awfully clever?"

"I ave answered tree questions, an darr'is enough,"
  Said iz dad; "do'n give yourself airs!
D'you tink I can lissen all day to such stuff?
  Be off, or I'll kick you downstairs!"

"Darr'is not said right," said de Caterpilla.

"Not *quite* right, I'm afraid," said Alice timidly: "Some o de werds ave got altered."

"Irr'is wrong from beginnin to end," said de Caterpilla decidedly, an der was silence for some minutes.

De Caterpilla was de ferst to speak., "What size d'you wanna be?" irr'asked.

"Oh, I ain't boddered as to size, "Alice astily replied; "ony one does'n like changin all de time, you know."

"I *don't* know," said de Caterpilla.

Alice said nothin: she'd never been so contradicted in all er life before, an she felt dat she was losin er rag.

"Are you appy now, den?" said de Caterpilla.

"Well, I'd like to be a *little* bigger, Ser, if you would'n mind, like," said Alice: "tree inches is such a wretched ight to be."

"Irr'is a very good ight indeed!" said de Caterpilla angrily, rearin itself upright as it spoke (i'was exackly tree inches igh).

"Burr'I'm not used to it!" pleaded poor Alice in a piteous tone. An she tought to erself, "I wish de creatchers would'n be so easily werked up!"

"You'll get used to it in time," said de Caterpilla; an it put de ookah in to its mout an began smokin again.

Dis time Alice waited patiently until it chose to speak again. In a minute or two de Caterpilla took de ookah ourr'of its mout an yawned once or twice, an shuwk itself. Den it got down off de mushroom an crawled away into de grass, merely remarkin as it went, "One side will make you grow taller, an de udder side will make you grow shorter."

"One side o *what?* De udder side o *what?*" tought Alice to erself.

"Of de mushroom," said de Caterpilla, just as if she'd asked it aloud; an in anudder momint i'was ourr'o sight.

Alice remained luwkin toughtfully at de mushroom for a minute, tryin to make out which were de two sides of it; an as i'was perfeckly round, she found irr'a dead ard question. Owever, at last she stretched er arms round irr'as far as dey would go, an broke off a birr'o de edge wid each and.

"An now which is which?" she said to erself, an nibbled a little o de right-and bit to try de effect: de next momint she felt a violint blow unnerneat er chin: irr'ad struck er foot!

She was dead scared by dis dead sudden change, but she felt der weren't no time to lose, as she was shrinkin dead fast: so she set to werk at once to eat some o de udder bit. Er chin was pressed so closely against er foot, dat der was ardly room to open er mout; but she did irr'at last, an manidged to swallie a morsel o de left-and bit.

"Come, me ead's free at last!" said Alice made-up-like, which changed into alarm in anudder momint, when she found darr'er shoulders were nowhere to be found: all she could see, when she luwked down, was a dirty great big long lorr'o neck, which seemed to rise like a stalk ourr'of a sea o green leaves dat lay far below er.

"What *can* all dat green stuff be?" said Alice. "An where've me shoulders got to? An oh, me poor ands, ow come I caan't see youse?" She was movin dem about as she spoke, but nothin seemed to appen, except a little shakin among de distint green leaves.

As der seemed to be no chance o gerrin er ands up to er ead, she tried to gerr'er ead down to *dem*, an was made up to find dat er neck would bend about easily in any direction, like a serpent. She'd just succeeded in kervin it down in a lovely zigzag, an was goin to dive in among de leaves, which she found to be nothin but de tops o de trees unner which she'd been wandrin, when a sharp iss made er draw back in a urry: a large pigeon ad flown into er face, an was beatin er violintly wid its wings.

"Serpent!" screamed de Pigeon.

"I'm *norr*'a serpent!" said Alice dead peeved. "Lemme alone!"

"Serpent, I say again!"repeated de Pigeon, burr'in a more subdued tone, an added wid a kind o sob, "I've tried every way, but nothin seems to suit dem!"

"I aven't de least idea what you're on about," said Alice.

"I've tried de roots o trees, an I've tried banks, an I've tried edges," de Pigeon wenn on, widout attendin to er, "but dose serpents! Der's no pleasin dem!"

Alice was more an more puzzled, but she tought der was no use in sayin anytin more till de Pigeon ad finished.

"As if it weren't trouble enough atchin de eggs," said de Pigeon, "burr'I muss be on de luwk-out for serpents night an day! Why, I ain't ad a wink o sleep dese tree weeks!"

"I'm dead sorry you've been boddered," said Alice, oo was beginnin to see wharr'it meant, like.

"An just as I'd taken de ighest tree in de wood," wenn on de Pigeon, raisin its voice to a shriek, "an just as I was tinkin I should be free o dem at last, dey gorra come wrigglin down ourr'o de sky! Ugh, Serpent!"

"Burr'I'm norr'a serpent, I tell you!" said Alice, "I'm a— I'm a—"

"Well! Wharr'are you?" said de Pigeon. "I can see you're tryin to invent sometin!"

"I—I'm a little gerl," said Alice, radder doubtfully, as she remembered de number o changes she'd gone truw dat day.

"Pull de udder one, den, eh!" said de Pigeon, wid a lorr'o contempt. "I seen a lorr'o little gerls in me time, but one wid a neck like dat! No, no! You're a serpent; an der's no use denyin it. I suppose you'll be tellin me next dat you never tasted an egg!"

"I *ave* tasted eggs, certainly," said Alice, oo was a dead truthful kid; "but little gerls eat eggs quite as much as serpents do, you know."

"I do'n believe it," said de Pigeon; "burr'if dey do, why, den dey're a kind o serpent: dat's all I can say."

Dis was such a new idea to Alice, dat she was quite silent for a minute or two, which gave de Pigeon de oppertchunity of addin, "You're luwkin for eggs, I know *dat* well enough; an what does it marrer to me whedder you're a little gerl or a serpent?"

"It marrers a lot to *me*," said Alice astily; "burr'I'm not luwkin for eggs, as it appens; an, if I was, I should'n want *yours*: I do'n like dem raw."

"Well gerr'out off it den!" said de Pigeon in a dead narky tone, as it settled down again in its nest. Alice crouched down among de trees as well as she could, for er neck kept catchin in de branches, an every now an den she ad to stop an untwist it. After a while she remembered dat she still eld de pieces o mushroom in er ands, an she set to werk very carefly, nibblin ferst at one an den de udder, an growin sometimes taller, an sometimes shorter, until she'd succeeded in bringin erself down to er usual ight.

I'was so long since she'd been anytin like de right size, darr'it felt quite strange at ferst; but she got used to it in a few minutes, an began tawkin to erself, as usual, "Come, der's alf me plan done already! Ow puzzlin all dese changes are! I'm never sure wharr'I'm gonna be, from one minute to de next! Owever, I've got back to me right size: de next ting is, to gerr'into dat beautiful gardin—ow *is* dat to be done, I wunder?" As she said dis, she sunnly came upon an open place, wid a little ouse in it about four feet igh. "Ooever lives der," tought Alice, "irr'll never do to come up on dem *dis* size: why, I'd scared em ourr'o deir wits!" So she began nibblin at de right-and bit again, an din't ventcher to go near de ouse till she'd brought erself down to nine inches igh.

CHAPTER VI

Pig an Pepper

For a minute or two she stud luwkin at de ouse, an wundrin what to do next, when sunnly a footman in a lackey-suit came runnin ourr'o de wood—(she tought e was a footman cause e was decked out in a lackey-suit: udderwise, judgin by de luwk of iz face ony, she would ave called im a fish)—an rapped loudly at de door wid iz knuckles. I'was opened by anudder footman in a lackey-suit, wid a round face, an big eyes like a frog; an both footmen, Alice noticed, ad powdered air dat kerled all over deir eads. She felt dead curious to know wharr'i'was all about, an crept a little way out o de wood to lissen.

De Fish-Footman began by takin a great big lerrer from unner iz arm, nearly as big as imself, an dis e anded over to de udder, sayin in a solemn tone, "For de Duchess. An invitation from de Queen to play crokay." De Frog-Footman repeated in de same solemn tone, ony changin de order o de werds a little, "From de Queen. An invitation for de Duchess to play crokay."

Den dey both bowed low, an deir kerls got entangled togedder.

Alice laughed so much at dis, dat she ad to run back into de wood for fear o dem earin er; an, when next she peeped out, de Fish-Footman was gone, an de udder was sittin on de ground near de door, starin stupidly up inte de sky.

Alice went timidly up to de door, an knocked.

"Der's no sorr'o use in knockin," said de Footman, "an dat for two reasons. Ferst, cause I'm on de same side as you is: secondly, cause dey're makin so much noise inside, no one could possibly ear you." And certainly der was a most extra-ordinry noise goin on widdin—a constant owlin an sneezin, an every now an den a great crash, as if a dish or kettle ad been broken to bits.

"Please, den," said Alice, "ow am I gonna gerr'in, like?"

"Der might be some sense in your knockin," de Footman wenn on, widout attendin to er, "if we ad de door between us. For instance, if you were *inside*, you might knock, an I could let you out, you know." E was luwkin up inte de sky all de time e was speakin, an dis Alice tought dead bad-mannered. "But peraps e caan't elp it," she said to erself; "Iz eyes are so *very* near de top of iz ead. Burr'at any rate e might answer questions—Ow am I to gerr'in?" she repeated aloud.

"I shall sit ere," de Footman remarked, "till tomorra—"

At dis momint de door o de ouse opened, an a large plate came skimmin out, straight at de Footman's ead: it just grazed iz nose, an broke to pieces against one o de trees be'ind im.

"—or next day, maybe," de Footman wenn on in de same tone, exackly as if nothin ad appened.

"Ow am I to gerr'in?" asked Alice again, in a louder tone.

"*Are* you to gerr'in arr'all?" said de Footman. "Dat's de ferst question, you know."

I'was, no doubt: ony Alice din't like bein tole so. "It's really dreadful," she muttered to erself, "de way all de creatchers argue. It's enough to drive one crazy!"

De Footman seemed to tink dis a good oppertchunity for repeatin iz remark wid variations. "I shall sit ere," e said, "on an off, for days an days."

"But wharr'am *I* to do?" said Alice.

"Anytin you like," said de Footman, an began whistlin.

"Oh, der's no use in tawkin to im," said Alice despratly: "E's a right idiot, e is!" An she opened de door an wenn in.

De door led right inte a large kitchin, which was full o smoke from one end to de udder: de Duchess was sittin on a tree-legged stool in de miggle, nersin a baby: de cuwk was leanin over de fire, sterrin a large cauldron which seemed to be full o soup.

"Der's certainly too much pepper in dat soup!" Alice said to erself, as well as she could for sneezin.

Der was certainly to much of it in de *air*. Even de Duchess sneezed occasionly; an as for de baby, i'was sneezin an owlin alternately widout a momint's pause. De ony two creatchers in de kitchin dat *din't* sneeze, were de cuwk, an a large moggy, which was lyin on de arth an grinnin from ear to ear.

"Please would you tell me," said Alice a little timidly, for she was'n quite sure whedder i'was good manners for er to speak ferst, "why your moggy grins like dat?"

"It's a Cheshire-Cat," said de Duchess, "an dat's why. Pig!"

She said de last werd wid such sudden violince dat Alice quite jumped; but she saw in anudder momint darr'i'was addressed to de baby, an not to er, so she took art, an wenn on again:—

"I din't know dat Cheshire-Cats allus grinned; in fack, I din't know dat moggies *could* grin."

"Dey all can," said de Duchess; "an most o dem do."

"I do'n know any dat do," Alice said dead polite-like, feelin quite chuffed to ave gorr'in to a conversation.

"You do'n know much," said de Duchess, "an dat's no joke neider."

Alice din't like de tone o dis arr'all, an tought it would be as well to tawk about sometin else. While she was tryin to tink o sometin, de cuwk took de cauldron off de fire, an set to werk at once trowin everytin widdin er reach at de Duchess an de baby—de fire-irons came ferst; den follied a shower o saucepans, plates, an dishes. De Duchess took no notice o dem even when dey itt er; an de baby was owlin so much already, darr'i'was quite impossible to say whedder de blows urt irr'or not.

"Oh, *please* mind what you're doin"! cried Alice, jumpin up an down in a right tizzy. "Oh, der goes iz *precious* nose!" as an unusually large saucepan flew close by it, an almost carried irr'off.

"If everybody minded deir own business," de Duchess said, in a oarse growl, "de werld would go round a good deal faster dan it does."

"Which would *not* be an advantidge," said Alice, oo felt dead appy to gerr'a chance o showin off a birr'of er knowlidge. "Just tink what werk i'would make wid de day an night! You see, de earth takes twenny-four hours to tern round on its axis—"

"Tawkin of axes," said de Duchess, "chop off er ead!"

Alice glanced radder anxiously at de cuwk, to see if she meant to take de int; but de cuwk was busily sterrin de soup; an din't seem to be earwiggin, so she wenn on again: "Twenny-four hours, I *tink*; or is it twelve? I—"

"Oh, do'n bodder me!" said de Duchess. "I never could abide figgers!" An wid dat she began nersin er kid again, singin a sorr'o lullaby to it as she did so, an givin irr'a violint shake at de end of every line:—

> "Speak roughly to your little boy,
>   An beat im when e sneezes:
> E ony does it to annoy,
>   Because e knows it teases."

CHORUS
(In which de cuwk and de baby joined):—
"Wow! wow! wow!"

While de Duchess sang de second verse o de song, she kept tossin de baby violintly up an down, an de poor little ting owled so, dat Alice could ardly ear de werds:—

> "I speak severely to me boy,
>   I beat im when e sneezes;
> For e can toroughly enjoy
>   De pepper when e pleases!"

CHORUS
"Wow! wow! wow!"

"Ere! You may nerse irr'a bit, if you like!" de Duchess said to Alice, flingin de baby arr'er as she spoke. "I muss go an get ready to play crokay wid de Queen," an she urried ourr'o de room. De cuwk trew a fryin-pan after er as she went, burr'it just missed er.

Alice caught de baby wid some difficulty, as i'was a queer-shaped little creacher, an eld ourr'its arms an legs all which ways, "just like a star-fish," tought Alice. De poor little ting was snortin like a steam-engine when she caught it, an kept doublin itself up an straightenin itself ourr'again, so dat altogedder, for de ferst minute or two, i'was all she could do to keep old of it.

As soon as she ad made out de proper way o nersin it (which was to twist irr'up in a sorr'o knot, an den keep tight old of its right ear an left foot, so as to stop it undoin itself), she carried irr'out into de open air. "If I do'n take dis kid away wid me," tought Alice, "dey're sure to kill it in a day or two: would'n it be murder to leave it be'ind?" She said de last werds out loud, an de little ting grunted in reply (irr'ad left off sneezin by dis time). "Do'n grunt," said Alice; "darr'ain't de proper way arr'all of expressin yourself."

De baby grunted again, an Alice luwked dead anxiously into its face to see what was de marrer wid it. Der was no doubt irr'ad a *very* terned up nose, much more like a snout dan a real nose: also its eyes were gerrin dead small for a baby: Alice din't like de luwk of it arr'all. "But peraps i'was ony sobbin," she tought, an luwked into its eyes again, to see if der was any tears.

No, der were no tears. "If you're gonna tern into a pig, me love," said Alice, seriously, "I'll ave nothin more to do wid you. Mind now!" De poor little ting sobbed again (or grunted, i'was impossible to say which), an dey wenn on for some while in silence.

Alice was just beginnin to tink to erself, "Now, wharr'am I to do wid dis creatcher, when I gerr'it ome?" when it grunted again so ard, dat she luwked down into its face in some alarm, Dis time der could be no mistake abourr'it: i'was neider more or less dan a pig, an she tought darr'i'would be dead daft to carry irr'any ferder.

So she set de little creatcher down, an felt quite relieved to see it trot away quietly into de wood. "If irr'ad grown up," she said to erself, "i'would ave made a dead ugly kid: burr'it makes a dead andsome pig, I tink." An she began tinkin over udder kids she knew, oo might do very well as pigs, an was just sayin to erself "if one ony knew de right way to change dem—" when she was a little startled by seein de Cheshire-Cat sittin on a bow of a tree a few yards off.

De Moggy ony grinned when it saw Alice. It luwked pally-like, she tought: still it did ave very long claws an loads o teeth, so she felt it best to give it a wide berth.

"Cheshire-Puss," she began radder timidly, as she din't know whedder i'would like de name: owever irr'ony grinned a little wider. "Come, it's pleased so far," tought Alice, an she wenn on. "Would you tell me, please, which way I oughta go from ere?"

"Dat depends a lorr'on were you wanna get to," said de Moggy.

"I do'n much care where—" said Alice.

"Den it do'n marrer which way you go," said de Moggy.

"—so long as I get *somewhere*," Alice added as an explanation.

"Oh, you're sure to do dat," said de Moggy: "If you ony wawk for long enough."

Alice felt dat she could'n argue wid dat, so she tried anudder question. "What sorr'o people live round ere?"

"In *dat* direction," de Moggy said, wavin its right paw round, "lives a Atter: an in *dat* direction," wavin de udder paw, "lives a March Are. Visit eider you like: dey're both mad."

"Burr'I do'n wanna go among mad people, "Alice remarked.

"Oh, you caan't elp dat," said de Moggy: "we're all mad ere. I'm mad. You're mad."

" Ow d'you know I'm mad?" said Alice.

"You gorra be," said de Moggy, "or you would'n ave come ere."

Alice din't tink dat proved it arr'all; owever, she wenn on: "An ow d'you know dat you're mad?"

"Te begin wid," said de Moggy, "a dog's not mad. You grant dat?"

"I suppose so," said Alice.

"Well den," de Moggy wenn on, "you see a dog growls when it's angry, an wags its tail when it's pleased. Now *I* growl when I'm pleased, an wag me tail when I'm angry. Derfore I'm mad."

"*I* call it perrin, not growlin," said Alice.

"Call it what you like," said de Moggy. "D' you play crokay wid de Queen to-day?"

"I'd love to," said Alice, "burr'I ain't been invited yet."

"You'll see me der," said de Moggy, an vanished.

Alice was'n much suprised at dis, she was gerrin so well used to queer tings appenin. While she were still luwkin at de place were irr'ad been, it sunnly appeared again.

"By-de-bye, what became o de baby?" said de Moggy. "I'd nearly forgot to ask."

"It terned into a pig, " Alice answered dead quietly, just as if de Moggy ad come back in a natchural way.

"I tought i'would," said de Moggy, an vanished again.

Alice waited a bit, alf expectin to see irr'again, burr'it din't appear, an after a minute or two she wawked on in de direction in which de March Are was said to live. "I've seen atters before," she said to erself: "de March Are will be de most intrestin, an peraps, as it's May, it wo'n be ravin mad—at least norr'as mad as i'was in March." As she said dis, she

luwked up, an der was de Moggy again, sittin on a branch of a tree.

"Did you say 'pig', or 'fig'?" said de Moggy.

"I said 'pig'," replied Alice; "an I wish you would'n keep comin an goin so sunnly: you're makin me go dead giddy!"

"All right," said de Moggy; an dis time it vanished quite slowly, startin wid de end of its tail, an endin wid de grin, which remained some time after de rest of irr'ad gone.

"Well! I've offen seen a moggy widout a grin," tought Alice; "burr'a grin widout a moggy! It's de most curious ting I ever saw in all me life!"

She ad'n gone much ferder before she came in sight o de ouse o de March Are: she tought it muss be de right ouse, cause de chimbleys were shaped like ears an de roof was tatched wid fer. I'was so large a ouse, dat she din't wanna go nearer till she'd nibbled some more o de left-and birr'o mushroom, an raised erself to about two feet igh: even den she wawked towards it dead timidly, sayin to erself "Suppose it should be ravin mad after all! I almost wish I'd gone to see de Atter instead!"

CHAPTER VII

A Mad Tea-Party

*D*er was a table set out unner a tree in front o de ouse, an de March Are an de Atter were avin deir tea arr'it: a Dormouse was sittin between dem, fast asleep, an de udder two were usin irr'as a cushion, restin deir elbas on it, an tawkin over its ead. "Very uncomftable for de Dormouse," tought Alice; "ony it's asleep, an I suppose it do'n mind."

De table was a large one, burr'all tree were crowded togedder at one corner of it. "No room! No room!" Dey cried out when dey saw Alice comin. "Der's *plenny* o room!" said Alice indignintly, an she sat down in a large arm-chair at one end o de table.

"Ave some wine," de March Are said in an encouridgin tone.

Alice luwked all round de table but der weren't nothin on it but tea.

"I do'n see any wine," she remarked.

"Der ain't none," said de March Are.

"Den i'was'n very civil o you to offer it," said Alice angrily.

"I'was'n very civil o you to sit down widout bein invited," said de March Are.

"I din't know i'was *your* table," said Alice: "It's laid out for a lot more dan tree."

"Your air wants cuttin," said de Atter. E ad been gozzin at Alice for some time wid great curiosity, an dis was iz ferst speech.

"You should lern not to be so personal," Alice said wid some severity: "it's dead rude."

De Atter opened iz eyes very wide on earin dis; burr'all e *said* was "Why is a raven like a writin-desk?"

"Come, we shall ave some fun now!" tought Alice. "I'm glad dey've begun askin riddles—I believe I can guess dat," she added aloud.

"D'you mean dat you tink you can find out de answer to it," said de March Are.

"Exackly so," said Alice.

"Den you should say what you mean," de March Are wenn on.

"I do," Alice astily replied; "at least—at least I mean wharr'I say—dat's de same ting, you know."

"Not de same ting a bit!" said de Atter. "Why, you might just as well say dat 'I see wharr'I eat' is de same ting as 'I eat wharr'I see'!"

"You might just as well say dat," said de March Are, "dat 'I like wharr'I get' is de same ting as 'I get wharr'I like'!"

"You might just as well say," added de Dormouse, which seemed to be tawkin in its sleep, "dat 'I breathe when I sleep' is de same ting as 'I sleep when I breathe'!"

"Irr'*is* de same ting wid you," said de Atter, an ere de conversation dropped, an de all sat silent for a minute, while Alice tought over all she could remember about ravens an writin-desks, which weren't much.

De Atter was de ferst to break de silence. "What day o de month is it?" e said, ternin to Alice: e ad taken iz watch ourr'of iz pockit, an was luwkin arr'it uneasily, shakin irr'every now an den, an oldin it to iz ear.

Alice considered a little, an den said, "De fourth."

"Two days wrong!" sighed de Atter. "I tole you butter would'n suit de werks!" e added, luwkin angrily at de March Are.

"I'was de *best* butter," de March Are meekly replied.

"Yeah, but some crums must ave gorr'in as well," de Atter grumbled. "You should'n ave purr'it in wid de bread-knife."

De March Are took de watch an luwked arr'it gloomily; den e dipped irr'in iz cup o tea, an luwked arr'it again: burr'e could'n tink o nothin to say berrer dan iz ferst remark, "I'was de *best* butter, you know."

Alice ad been luwkin over iz shoulder wid some curiosity. "Wharr'a funny watch!" she remarked." It tells de day o de month, an does'n tell what o'clock irr'is!"

"Why should it?" muttered de Atter. "Does your *watch* tell you what year irr'is?"

"O course not," Alice replied very readily: "but dat's cause it stays de same year for such a long time togedder."

"Which is just de case wid *mine*," said de Atter.

Alice felt dead puzzled. De Atter's remark seemed to er to ave no sorr'o meanin in it, an yerr'i'was certainly Scouse. "I do'n quite unnerstand you," she said, as politely as she could.

"De Dormouse is asleep again," said de Atter, an e poured a little ot tea on its nose.

De Dormouse shook its ead impatiently, an said, widout openin its eyes, "Of course, o course: just wharr'I was goin to remark meself."

"Ave you guessed de riddle yet?" de Atter said, ternin to Alice again.

"Nah, I give irr'up," Alice replied. "What's de answer?"

"I aven't de foggiest idea," said de Atter.

"Nor I," said de March Are.

Alice sighed wearily. "I tink you might do sometin berrer wid de time," she said, "dan wastin irr'in askin riddles darr'ave no answers."

"If you knew Time as well as I do," said de Atter, "you would'n tawk about wastin *it*. It's *im*."

"I do'n know what you mean," said Alice.

"O course you do'n," de Atter said, tossin iz ead contemptuously. "I dare say you never even spoke to Time!"

"Peraps not," Alice cautiously replied; "burr'I know I ave to beat time when I lern music."

"Ah! Dat accounts for it," said de Atter. "E wo'n stand beating. Now, if you ony kept on iz good side, e'd do almost anytin you liked wid de clock. For instance, suppose i'was nine o'clock in de mornin, just time to begin lessins: you'd ony ave to whisper a int to Time, an round goes de clock in a twinklin! Alf past one, time for dinner!"

("I ony wish it were," de March Are said to itself in a whisper.)

"Dat would be grand, certainly," said Alice toughtfully; "but den—I should'n be ungry for it, you know, like."

"Norr'at ferst, peraps," said de Atter: "but you could keep it to alf past one as long as you liked."

"Is dat de way *you* manidge?" Alice asked.

De Atter shook iz ead mournfully. "Norr'I!" e replied. "We quarrelled last March—just before *e* went mad, you know—" (pointin wid iz teaspoon at de March Are) "—-i'was at de great concert given by de Queen of Arts, an I ad to sing

'Twinkle, twinkle, little bat!
Ow I wunder what you're at!'

You know de song, do you, eh?"

"I've eard sometin like it," said Alice.

"It goes on, you know," de Atter continued, "in dis way:—

'Up above de werld you fly,
Like a tea-tray in de sky.
Twinkle, twinkle—'"

Ere de Dormouse shook itself an began singin in its sleep *"Twinkle, twinkle, twinkle, twinkle—"* an wenn on so long dat dey ad to pinch it to make it stop.

"Well, I'd ardly finished de ferst verse," said de Atter, "when de Queen bawled out, 'E's murdrin de time! Off wid iz ead!'"

"Ow dreadfully savidge!" exclaimed Alice.

"An ever since dat," de Atter wenn on in a mournful tone, "E wo'n do a ting I ask! It's allus six o'clock now."

A bright idea came into Alice's ead. "Is dat de reason so many tea-tings are purr'out ere?" she asked.

"Yiss, dat's it," said de Atter wid a sigh: "It's allus tea-time, an we've no time to wash de tings between whiles."

"Den you keep movin round, I suppose?" said Alice.

"Exackly so," said de Atter: "as de tings get used up."

"But wharr'appens when you come to de beginnin again?" Alice ventchered to ask.

"Suppose we change de subjeck," de March Are innerrupted, yawnin. "I'm gerrin tired o dis. I vote de young gerl tells us a story."

"I'm afraid I do'n know one," said Alice, radder alarmed at de proposal.

"Den de Dormouse shall!" dey both cried. "Wake up, Dormouse!" An dey pinched irr'on both sides at once.

De Dormouse slowly opened its eyes. "I was'n asleep," it said in a oarse, feeble voice, "I eard every werd you lot were sayin."

"Tell us a story!" said de March Are.

"Yiss, please do, lar!" pleaded Alice.

"An be quick abourr'it," added de Atter, "or you'll be asleep again before it's done."

"Once upon a time der were tree sisters," de Dormouse began in a great urry; "an deir names were Elsie, Lacie, an Tillie; an dey lived at de bottom of a well—"

"What did dey live on?" said Alice, oo allus took a great intrest in questions of eatin an drinkin.

"Dey lived on treacle," said de Dormouse, after tinkin a minute or two. "Day could'n ave done dat, you know," Alice said dead gentle-like, "dey'd ave been ill."

"So dey were," said de Dormouse; "*very* ill."

Alice tried a little to fancy to erself what such a extraordinry way o livin would be like, burr'it puzzled er too much: so she wenn on: "But why did dey live at de bottom of a well?"

"Take some more tea," de March Are said to Alice, earnestly.

"I've ad nothin yet," Alice replied in a offended tone: "so I caan't take more."

"You mean you caan't take *less*," said de Atter: "it's dead easy to take *more* dan nothin."

"Nobody asked *your* opinion," said Alice.

"Oo's makin personal remarks now?" de Atter asked triumphantly.

Alice din't quite know what to say to dis: so she elped erself to some tea an bread-an-butter, an den terned to de Dormouse, an repeated er question. "Why did dey live at de bottom of a well?"

De Dormouse again took a minute or two to tink abourr'it, and den said, "I'was a treacle-well."

"Der's no such ting!" Alice was gerrin dead narked, but de Atter an de March Are went "Sh! Sh!" an de Dormouse sulkily remarked "If you caan't be civil, you'd berrer finish de story for yourself."

"No, please go on!" Alice said, dead umble. "I wo'n inner-rupt you again. I dare say der may be one.

"One, indeed!" said de Dormouse indignintly, "Owever, e consented to go on. "An so dese tree little sisters—dey were lernin to draw, you know—"

"What did dey draw?" said Alice, quite forgettin er promise.

"Treacle," said de Dormouse, widout considrin arr'all, dis time.

"I wanna clean cup," innerrupted de latter: "Let's all move one place on."

E moved on as e spoke, an de Dormouse follied im: de March Are moved into de Dormouse's place, an Alice radder unwillinly took de place o de March Are. De Atter was de ony one oo gorr'any advantidge from de change; an Alice was a good deal werse off dan before, as de March Are ad just upset de milk-jug into iz plate.

Alice din't wish to offend de Dormouse again, so she began very cautiously: "Burr'I do'n unnerstand. Where did dey draw de treacle from?"

"You can draw water ourr'of a water-well," said de Atter; "so I should tink you could draw treacle ourr'of a treacle-well—eh, stupid?"

"But dey were *in* de well," Alice said to de Dormouse, not choosin to notice dis last remark.

"Of course dey were, "said de Dormouse: "well in."

Dis answer so confused poor Alice, dat she let de Dormouse go on for some time widout innerruptin it.

"Dey were lernin to draw," de Dormouse when on, yawnin an rubbin its eyes, for i'was gerrin dog-tired; "an dey drew all sorts o tings—every ting dat begins wid a M—"

"Why wid a M?" said Alice.

"Why not?" said de March Are.

Alice was silent.

De Dormouse ad closed its eyes by dis time, an was goin off into a doze; but, on bein pinched by de Atter; it woke up again wid a little shriek, an wenn on: "—dat begins wid a M, such as mousetraps, an de moon, an memry, an muchness— you know, you say tings are 'much of a muchness'—d'you ever see such a ting as a drawin of a muchness?"

"Really, now you're askin," said Alice, dead confused, "I do'n tink—"

"Den you should'n tawk," said de Atter.

Dis birr'o rudeness was more dan Alice could take: she gorr'up in a big uff, an wawked off: de Dormouse fell asleep instintly, on neider o de udders took de least birr'o notice of er goin, dough she luwked back once or twice, alf opin dat dey would call after er: de last time she saw dem, dey were tryin to put de Dormouse into de teapot.

"Arr'any rate I'll never go der again!" said Alice, as she picked er way trew de wood, "It's de stupidest tea-party I ever was at in all me life!"

Just as she said dis, she seen dat one o de trees ad a door leadin right into it. "Dat's a bit curious!" she tought. "Burr'everytin's curious to-day. I tink I mighrr'as well go in at once." An in she went.

Once more she found erself in de long all, on close to de little glass table. "Now, I'll manidge berrer dis time," she said to erself, an began by takin de little golden key, an unlockin de door dat led into de gardin. Den she set to werk nibblin at de mushroom (she'd kept a piece of it in er pockit) till she was abourr'a foot igh, den she wawked down de little passidge: an den—she found erself at last in de lovely gardin, among de bright flower-beds an de cool fountains.

CHAPTER VIII

De Queen's Crokay-Ground

A large rose-tree stud near de entrance o de gardin: de roses growin on it were white, but der were tree gardiners arr'it, busily paintin dem red. Alice tought dis a very curious ting, an she went nearer to watch dem, she eard one o dem say, "Luwk out now, Five! Do'n go splashin paint over me like dat!"

"I could'n elp it," said Five, in a sulky tone. "Seven jogged me elba."

On which Seven luwked up an said "Dat's right, Five! Always blamin udders!"

"*You* caan't tawk!" said Five. "I eard de Queen say ony yisterdy you deserved to be be'eaded."

"What for?" said de one oo ad spoke ferst.

"Dat's none o *your* business, Two!" said Seven.

"Yiss, irr'*is* iz business!" said Five. "An I'll tell im—i'was for bringin de cuwk tewlip-roots instead of onions."

Seven flung down iz brush, an ad just begun "Well, of all de unjust tings—" when e spotted Alice, as she stud watchin dem, an e checked imself sunnly: de udders luwked round also, an all o dem bowed low.

"Would you tell me, lads," said Alice, a bit timid-like, "why you're paintin dose roses?"

Five an Seven said nothin, but luwked at Two. Two began, in a low voice, "Why, de ting is, you see, gerl, dis ere oughta ave been a *red* rose-tree, an we purr'a white one by mistake, an if de Queen was to find out, we should all ave our eads cut off, you know. So you see, gerl, were doin our best, afore she comes, to—" At dis momint, Five, oo'd been anxiously luwkin across de gardin, called out "De Queen! De Queen!" an de tree gardiners instintly trew demselves flat upon deir faces. Der was a sound o many footsteps, an Alice luwked round, eager to see de Queen.

Ferst came ten sodjers carryin clubs: dese were all shaped like de tree gardiners, oblong an flat, wid deir ands an feet at de corners: next de ten courtiers: dese were ornaminted all over wid diamonds, an wawked two an two, as de sodjers did. After dese came de royal kids: der were ten o dem, an de little dears came jumpin merrily along, and in and, in couples: dey were all ornamented wid arts. Next came de guests, mostly Kings an Queens, an among dem Alice recognized de White Rabbit: i'was tawkin in a urried nervous manner, smilin at every ting dat was said, an went by widout noticin er. Den follied de Knave of Arts, carryin de King's crown on a crimson velvit cushion; an, last of all in dis grand procession, came DE KING AN DE QUEEN OF ARTS.

Alice was radder doubtful whedder she ought not to lie down on er face like de tree gardiners, but she could'n remember ever avin eard o such a rule at processions; "an besides, what would be de use of a procession," tought she, "if people ad all to lie down on deir faces, so dey could'n see it?" So she stud where she was, an waited.

When de procession came opposite to Alice, dey all stopped an luwked arr'er, an de Queen said, severely "Oo is dis?" She said it to de Knave of Arts, oo ony bowed an smiled in reply.

"Idiot!" said de Queen, tossin er ead impatiently; an, ternin to Alice, she when on: What's your name, kiddo?"

"Me name is Alice, so please your Majisty," said Alice dead polite; but she added, to erself, "Why, dey're ony a pack o cards, after all. I need'n be afraid o dem!"

"An oo are *dese*?" said de Queen, pointin to de tree gardiners oo were lyin round de rose-tree; for, you see, as dey were lyin on deir faces, an de pattern on deir backs was de same as de rest o de pack she could not tell whedder dey were gardiners, or sodjers, or courtiers, or tree of er own kids.

"Ow should *I* know," said Alice, suprised arr'er own couridge. "It's no business o *mine*."

De Queen terned crimson wid fury, an, after glarin arr'er for a momint like a wild beast, began screamin "Off wid er ead! Off wid—"

"Nonsense!" said Alice, very loudly an decidedly, an de Queen was silent.

De King laid iz and upon er arm, an timidly said "Consider, me love: she's ony a kid!"

De Queen terned angrily away from im, an said to de Knave "Tern em over!"

De Knave did so, dead carefly, wid one foot.

"Gerr'up!" said de Queen in a shrill, loud voice, an de tree gardiners instantly jumped up, an began bowin to de King, de Queen, de royal kids, an everybody else.

"Leave off dat!" screamed de Queen. "You make me giddy." An den, ternin to de rose-tree, she wenn on "what *ave* you been doin ere?"

"May it please your Majisty," said Two, in a very umble tone, goin down on one knee as e spoke. "We was tryin—"

"*I* see!" said de Queen, oo'd meanwhile been examinin de roses. "Off wid deir eads!" an de procession moved on, tree o de sodjers remained be'ind to exeecute de unfortchunate gardiners, oo ran to Alice for protection.

"I'll see dey do'n urt you, lads; you wo'n lose your eads, while I'm ere!" said Alice, an she purr'em into a large flower-pot dat stud near. De tree sodjers wundered about for a minute or two, luwkin for dem, an den quietly marched off after de udders.

"Are deir eads off?" shouted de Queen.

"Deir eads are gone, if it please your Majisty!" de sodjers shouted in reply.

"Dat's right!" shouted de Queen. "Can you play crokay?"

De sodjers were silent, an luwked arr'Alice, as de question was evidently meant for er.

"Yiss!" shouted Alice.

"Come on, den!" roared de Queen, an Alice joined de procession, wundrin very much what would appen next.

"It's a lovely day!" said a timid voice arr'er side. She was wawkin by de White Rabbit, oo was peepin anxiously into er face.

"Very," said Alice. "Where's de Duchess?"

"Ush! Ush!" said de Rabbit in a low urried tone. E luwked anxiously over iz shoulder as e spoke, an den raised imself upon tiptoe, purr'iz mout close to er ear, an whispered "She's unner sentince of exeecution."

"What for?" said Alice.

"Did you say 'Wharr'a pity!'?" de Rabbit asked.

"Nah, I din't," said Alice. "I do'n tink it's arr'all a pity. I said 'What for?'"

"She boxed de Queen's ears—" de Rabbit began. Alice gave a little scream o laughter. "Oh, ush!" de Rabbit whispered in a frightened tone. "De Queen will ear you! You see, she come dead late, an de Queen said—"

"Get to your places!" shouted de Queen in a voice o tunder, an people began runnin every which way, tumblin up against each udder: owever dey got settled down in a minute or two, an de game began.

Alice tought she'd never seen such a curious crokay-ground in er life: i'was all ridges an furras: de crokay balls were live edge-ogs, an de mallets live flamingoes, an de sodjers ad to double demselves up an stand on deir ands an feet, to make de arches.

De werst ting Alice found at ferst was in manidgin er flamingo: she succeeded in gerrin its body tucked away, comfy-like, unner er arm, wid its legs angin down, but genrally, just as she'd gorr'its neck nicely straightened out, an was goin to give de edge-og a blow wid its ead, i'would twist itself round an luwk up in er face, wid such a puzzled expression dat she could'n elp berstin out laughin; an, when she'd gorr'its ead down, an was goin to begin again, i'was very provokin to find dat de edge-og ad unrolled itself, an was in de act o crawlin away: besides all dis, der was genrally a ridge or a furra in de way whenever she wanted to send de edge-og to, an, as de doubled up sodjers were allus gerrin up an wawkin off to udder parts o de ground, Alice soon came to de conclusion darr'i'was a very difficult game indeed.

De players all played at once, widout takin terns, quarrellin all de time, an, fightin for de edge-ogs; an in no time arr'all de Queen was in a right ould temper, an went stampin about,

an shoutin "Off wid iz ead!" or "Off wid er ead!" about once
a minute.

Alice began to feel dead uneasy: sure, she ad'n yet ad a
barney wid de Queen, but she knew it might appen any
minute. "An den," tought she, "what would become o me?
Dey do'n alf like be'eadin people ere: its a wunder der's
anyone left alive!"

She was gozzin around for some way to escape, an wundrin
whedder she could gerr'away widout bein seen, when she
noticed a curious appearance in de air: it puzzled er a lorr'at
ferst, burr'after watchin irr'a minute or two she seen it was
a grin, an she said to erself "It's de Cheshire-Cat: now I shall
ave somebody to tawk to."

"Ow you doin?" said de Moggy, as soon as der was mout
enough for it to speak wid.

Alice waited till de eyes appeared, an den nodded. "It's no use speakin to it," she tought, "till its ears ave come, or at least one o dem." In anudder minute de ole ead appeared, an den Alice put down er flamingo, an began an account o de game, feelin dead glad she ad someone to lissen to er. De Moggy seemed to tink dat der was enough of it now in sight, an no more of it appeared.

"I do'n tink dey play fair, "Alice began, in radder a complainin tone, "an dey quarrel so bad you caan't ear yourself speak—an dey do'n seem to ave any sorr'o rules: or if der is, nobody takes any notice of em—an you've no idea ow confusin irr'is, all de tings bein alive: like, der's de arch I gorra go truw next wawkin abourr'at de udder end o de ground—an I should ave crokayed de Queens edge-og just now, ony it ran away when it saw im comin!"

"Ow d'you like de Queen?: said de Moggy in a low voice.

"Norr'at all," said Alice: "she's so extremely—" Just den she noticed dat de Queen was so close be'ind er, lissenin: so she when on "—likely to win, darr'it's ardly werth finishin de game."

De Queen smiled an passed on.

"Oo are you tawkin to?" said de King, comin up te Alice, an looking at de Moggy's ead wid great curiosity.

"It's a friend o mine—a Cheshire-Cat." said Alice: "Lemme innerduce it."

"I do'n like te luwk of it arr'all," said de King: "Owever, it may kiss me and if it likes."

"I'd radder not," de Moggy remarked.

"Do'n be cheeky," said de King, "an do'n luwk at me like dat!" E got be'ind Alice as e spoke.

"A Moggy may eyeball a king," said Alice. "I've read darr'in some buwk, burr'I do'n remember where."

"Well, it muss be removed," said de King very decidedly; an e called to de Queen, oo was passin at de momint, "Me love, I wish you would ave dis ere moggy removed!"

De Queen ad ony one way o sortin tings out, big or small. "Off wid iz ead!" she said widout even luwkin round.

"I'll get de exeecutioner meself," said de King eagerly, an e urried off.

Alice tought she mighrr'as well go back an see ow de game was goin on, an she eard de Queen's voice in de distance, screamin wid passion. She'd already eard er sentince tree o de players to be exeecuted for avin missed deir terns, an she din't like de luwk o tings arr'all, as de game was in such a mess dat she never knew when i'was er tern or not. So she when off in search of er edge-og.

De edge-og was avin a fight wid anudder edge-og, which seemed to Alice a good time for crokayin one o dem wid de udder: de ony ting was, darr'er flamingo was goin across to de udder side o de gardin, were Alice could see it tryin in a elpless sorr'o way to fly up into a tree.

By de time she'd caught de flamingo an broughrr'it back, de fight was over, an both de edge-ogs were ourr'o sight. "Burr'it does'n marrer much," tought Alice, "as all de arches are gone from dis side o de ground." .So she tucked irr'away unner er arm, so i'would'n gerr'away again, an went back to chinwag to er friend.

When she got back to de Cheshire-Cat, she was suprised to find quite a large crowd collected round it: der was a dispute goin on between de exeecutioner, de King, an de Queen, oo were all tawkin at once, while all de rest were quite silent, an luwked dead uncomftable.

De momint Alice appeared, she was asked by all tree to settle de question, an dey repeated deir arguments to er, dough, as dey all spoke at once, she found it dead ard to make out exackly what dey said.

De exeecutioner's argument was, dat you could'n cut off a ead unless der was a body to cut irr'off from: darr'e ad never ad to do such a ting before, an e was'n gonna begin arr'iz time o life.

De King's argument was dat anytin darr'ad a ead could be be'eaded, an dat you weren't to tawk nonsense.

De Queen's argument was dat, if sometin was'n done abourr'it dead quick-like, she'd ave everybody exeecuted, all round. (I'was dis last remark darr'ad made de ole lorr'o dem luwk so grave an anxious.)

Alice could tink o nothin else to say but "It belongs to de Duchess: you'd berrer ask er abourr'it."

"She's in prison," de Queen said to de exeecutioner; "fetch er ere." An de exeecutioner when off like an arra.

De Moggy's ead began fadin away de momint e was gone, an, by de time e come back wid de Duchess, irr'ad entirely disappeared: so de King an de exeecutioner ran wild up an down, luwkin for it, while de rest o de party went back to de game.

CHAPTER IX

De Mock Tertle's Story

"*Y*ou caan't tink ow glad I am to see you again, me ould mate!" said de Duchess, as she tucked er arm dead pally-like into Alice's, an dey wawked off togedder.

Alice was very glad to find er in a good mood, an tought to erself dat peraps i'was any o de pepper darr'ad made er so savidge when dey met in de kitchin.

"When *I'm* a Duchess," she said to erself (norr'in a very opeful tone, dough), "I wo'n ave any pepper in me kitchin *arr'all*. Soop does very well widout—Maybe it's allus pepper dat makes people ot-tempered," she wenn on, really pleased arr'avin found ourr'a new kind o rule, "an vinigar dat makes dem sour—an chamomile dat makes dem bitter—an—an barley sugar an such tings dat make kids sweet-tempered. I ony wish dat people knew *dat*: den dey would'n be so stingy abourr'it, you know—"

She'd quite forgotten de Duchess by dis time, an was a little startled when she eard er voice close to er ear. "You're tinkin about sometin, me gerl, an dat makes you forget to

84

tawk. I caan't tell you just now what de moral o dat is, burr'I shall remember it in a bit."

"Peraps irr'ain't got one, " Alice ventchered to remark.

"Tut, tut, kiddo!" said de Duchess. "Everytin's gorr'a moral, if ony you can find it." An she squeezed erself up closer to Alice's side as she spoke.

Alice din't like er keepin so close to er: ferst, cause she ad a face like de back of a bus; also, cause she was exackly de right ight to rest er chin on Alice's shoulder, an i'was an uncomftable sharp chin. Owever, she din't wanna be rude: so she purr'up wid irr'as best as she could.

"De game's goin a lot berrer now," she said, to keep de conversation goin.

"Dat's right," said de Duchess: "an de moral o darr'is—'Oh, 'tis love, 'tis love, dat makes de werld go round!'"

"Somebody said," Alice whispered, "darr'it's done by everybody mindin deir own business."

"Ah, well! It means much de same ting," said de Duchess, diggin er sharp little chin into Alice's shoulder as she added "an de moral o *darr*'is—'Take care o de sense, an de sounds will take care o demselves'."

"Ow fond she is o findin morals in tings!" Alice tought to erself.

"I dare say your wundrin why I do'n put me arm round your waist," de Duchess said, after a pause: "de reason is, darr'I'm doubtful about de temper o your flamingo. Shall I try de experimint?"

"E might bite," Alice cautiously replied, norr'at all anxious to ave de experimint tried.

"Dead right," said de Duchess: "flamingoes an mustid both bite. An de moral o darr'is—'Berds of a feadder flock togedder'."

"Ony mustid ain't a berd," Alice remarked.

"Righto, as usual," said de Duchess: "Wharr'a clear way you ave o purrin tings!"

"It's a minral, I *tink*," said Alice.

"Of course irr'is," said de Duchess, oo seemed ready to agree to everytin dat Alice said: "Der's a large mustid-mine near ere. An de moral o darr'is—'De more der is o mine, de less der is o yours'."

"Oh, I know!" exclaimed Alice, oo ad'n took a birr'o notice o de last remark. "It's a vedgetable. It do'n luwk like one burr'it is."

"I quite agree wid you," said de Duchess; "an de moral o darr'is—'Be what you would seem to be', or, if you'd like it put more simply—'Never imagine yourself not to to udderwise dan wharr'it mighrr'appear to udders dat what you were or mighrr'ave been was not udderwise dan what you ad been would ave appeared to be udderwise'."

"I'd know what you're on about," Alice said very politely, "if I'd writ it down; burr'I caan't quite get de ang of it de way you purr'it."

"Darr'ain't nothin to wharr'I could say if I wanted," de Duchess replied, in a pleased tone.

"Oh, you're all right, do'n bodder yourself to say irr'any longer dan dat," said Alice.

"Oh, do'n tawk about trouble!" said de Duchess. "I make you a present of everytin I've said as yet."

"A cheap sorr'o present," tought Alice. "I'm glad people don give berthday presents like dat!" But she din't dare say irr'out loud.

"Tinkin again?" de Duchess asked, wid anudder dig of er sharp chin.

"I've a right te tink," said Alice sharply, for she was beginnin to feel a little wurried.

"Just abourr'as much right," said de Duchess, "as pigs ave to fly; and de m—"

But ere, to Alice's great suprise, de Duchess's voice died away, even in de miggle of er favrite werd "moral", an de arm dat was linked into ers began to tremble. Alice luwked up, an der stud de Queen in front o dem, wid er arms folded, frownin like a tunderstorm.

"A fine day, your Majisty." de Duchess began in a low, weak voice.

"Now I give you fair warnin," shouted de Queen, stampin on de ground as she poke; "eider you or your ead muss be off, and darr'in about alf no time! Take your choice!"

De Duchess took er choice, an was gone in a momint.

"Let's gerr'on wid de game," de Queen said to Alice; an Alice was too much frightened to say a werd, but slowly follied er back to de crokay-ground.

De udder guests ad taken advantidge o de Queen's absince, an were restin in de shade: owever, de momint dey saw er, dey urried back to de game, de Queen merely sayin darr'a momint's delay would cost dem deir lives.

All de time dey were playin de Queen never left off quarrelin wid de udder players, an shoutin "Off wid iz ead!" or "Off wid er ead!" Dose oo she sentinced were taken into custidy by de sodjers, oo o course ad to leave off bein arches to do dis, so dat, by de end of alf an hour or so, der were no arches left, an all de players, except de King, de Queen, an Alice, were in custidy an unner sentince of exeecution.

Den de Queen left off, quite puffed, an said to Alice, "Ave you seen de Mock Tertle yet?"

"Nah," said Alice. "I do'n even know wharr'a Mock Tertle is."

"It's de ting Mock Tertle Soup is made from," said de Queen.

"I never saw one, or eard of one," said Alice.

"Come on, den," said de Queen, "an e shall tell you iz istry."

As dey wawked off togedder, Alice eard de King say in a low voice, to de compny genrally, "You're all pardoned." "Come, *dat's* a good ting!" she said to erself, for she ad felt quite un-appy at de number of exeecutions de Queen ad ordered.

Dead soon dey came upon a Gryphon, lyin fast asleep in de sun. (If you do'n know wharr'a Gryphon is, luwk at de pitchure.) "Up, lazy ting!" said de Queen, "an take dis young gerl to see de Mock Tertle, an to ear iz istry. "I gorra go back an see about some exeecutions I ordered"; an she wawked off, leavin Alice alone wid de Gryphon. Alice din't like de luwk arr'all o de creatcher, burr'on de ole she tought i'would be

just as safe to stay wid it as to go after dat savidge Queen: so
she waited.

De Gryphon sat up an rubbed iz eyes: den it watched de
Queen till she was ourr'o sight: den it chuckled. "What fun!"
said de Gryphon, alf to itself, alf to Alice.

"What *is* de fun?" said Alice.

"Why, *she,*" said de Gryphon. "It's all er fancy, dat: dey
never exeecutes nobody, you know. Come on!"

"De all say 'come on!' ere," tought Alice, as she went slowly
after it: "I never was so ordered about before, in all me life,
never!"

Dey ad'n gone far before dey saw de Mock Tertle in de
distance, sittin sad an lonely on a little ledge o rock, an, as
dey got nearer, Alice could ear im sighin as if iz art would
break. She felt dead sorry for im. "Wharr'is iz sorra?" she
asked de Gryphon. An de Gryphon answered, very nearly in
de same werds as before, "It's all iz fancy, dat: e ain't got no
sorra, you know. Come on!"

So dey wenn up to de Mock Tertle, oo luwked at dem wid large eyes full o tears, but said nothin.

"Dis ere young gerl," said de Gryphon, "she wants for to know your istry, she does."

"I'll tell it to er," said de Mock Tertle in a deep, olla tone. "Sit down, both o you, an do'n say a werd till I've finished—"

So dey sat down, an nobody spoke for some minutes. Alice tought to erself "I do'n see ow e can ever finish, if e do'n begin." But she ung on patiently.

"Once," said de Mock Tertle at last, wid a deep sigh, "I was a reel Tertle."

Dese werds were follied by a very long silence, broken ony by an occasional exclamation of "Hjckrrh!" from de Gryphon, an de constant eavy sobbin o de Mock Tertle. Alice was very nearly gerrin up an sayin "Ta, lar, for your intrestin story," but she could'n elp tinkin der *muss* be more to come, so she sat still an said nothin.

"When we was little," de Mock Tertle wenn on at last, more caamly, dough still sobbin a bit now an again, "we went to school in de sea. De teacher was a ould Tertle—we used to call im Tortoyse—"

"Why'd you call im Tortoyse, if e was'n one?" Alice asked.

"We called im Tortoyse cause e taught us," said de Mock Tertle angrily. "Really, your dead dull!"

"You oughta be ashamed o yourself for askin such a simple question," added de Gryphon; an den dey both sat silent an luwked at poor Alice, oo felt ready to sink into de earth. At last de Gryphon said to de Mock Tertle "Drive on, me ould pal! Do'n be all day abourr'it!", an e when on in dese werds:—

"Yiss, we went to school in de sea, dough you might'n believe it—"

"I never said I din't!" innerrupted Alice.

"You did," said de Mock Tertle.

"Old your tongue!" added de Gryphon, before Alice could speak again. De Mock Tertle wenn on.

"We ad de best of educations—in fack we went to school everyday—"

"*I've* been to a day-school, too," said Alice. "You need'n be as big-eaded as all dat."

"Wid extras?" asked de Mock Tertle, a bit anxiously.

"Yiss," said Alice: "We lernt French an music."

"An washin?" said de Mock Tertle.

"No chance, pal!" said Alice indignintly.

"Ah! Den your school must ave been dead last," said de Mock Tertle dead made up. "Now, at *ours*, dey ad, at de end o de bill 'French, music, *an washin*—extra.'"

"Ya could'n ave wanted it much," said Alice; "livin at de bottom o de sea."

"I could'n afford to lern it," said de Mock Tertle wid a sigh. "I ony took de reglar course."

"What was dat?" inquired Alice.

"Reelin an Writhin, o course, to begin wid," de Mock Tertle replied; "an den de diffrent branches o Rithmetik—Ambition, Distraction, Uglification, an Derision."

"I never eard of Uglification," Alice ventchered to say, "Wharr'is it?"

De Gryphon lifted up both of its paws in suprise. "Never eard of uglifyin!" irr'exclaimed. "You know what to beautify is, I suppose?"

"Yiss," said Alice doubtfully: "it means—to—make—anytin—prittier."

"Well, den," de Gryphon wenn on, "if you do'n know what to uglify is, you are a simpleton."

Alice din't feel encouridged to ask any more questions abourr'it; so she terned to de Mock Tertle, and said "Wharr'else did you ave to lern?"

"Well, der was Mystry," de Mock Tertle replied, countin off de subjecks on iz flappers, "Mystry, ancient an modern, wid Seography: den Drawlin—de Drawlin-master was a ould Conger-Eel, dat used to come once a week: *e* taught us Drawlin, Stretchin and Faintin in Coils."

"What was *dat* like?" said Alice.

"Well, I caan't show you, meself," de Mock Tertle said: "I'm too stiff. And de Gryphon never lernt it."

"Ad'n time," said de Gryphon. "I went to de classical master, dough. E was an ould crab, e was."

"I never went to im," de Mock Tertle said wid a sigh. "E taught Laughin an Grief, dey used to say."

"So e did, so e did," said de Gryphon, sighin in iz tern; an both creatchers id deir faces in deir paws.

"An ow m any hours a day did you do lessins?" said Alice, in a urry to change de subjeck.

"Ten hours de ferst day," said de Mock Tertle: "nine de next, an so on."

"Wharr'a curious plan!" exclaimed Alice.

"Dat's de reason dey're called lessins," de Gryphon remarked: "cause dey lessen from day to day."

Dis was quite a new idea to Alice, an she tought irr'over a bit before she made er next remark. "Den de eleventh day must ave been a ollyday?"

"Of course i'was," said de Mock Tertle.

"An ow did you manidge on de twelft?" Alice when on eagerly.

"Dat's enough about lessins," de Gryphon innerruptid in a very decided tone. "Tell er sometin about de games now."

CHAPTER X

De Lobster-Quadrille

De Mock Tertle sighed deeply, an drew de back o one flapper across iz eyes. E luwked arr'Alice an tried to speak, but, for a minute or two, sobs choked iz voice. "Same as if e ad a bone in iz troat," said de Gryphon; an it set to werk shakin im an punchin im in de back. At last de Mock Tertle recovered iz voice, an, wid tears runnin down iz cheeks, e wenn on again:—

"You may norr'ave lived much unner de sea—" ("I aven't," said Alice) "—an peraps you were never even innerduced to a lobster—" (Alice began to say "I once tasted—" but checked erself astily, an said "No, never—") "—so you ain't gorr'a clue wharr'a delightful ting a Lobster-Quadrille is!"

"No, you're right der, lar," said Alice. "What sorr'o dance is it?"

"Why," said de Gryphon, "you ferst form into a line along de sea-shore—"

"Two lines!" cried de Mock Tertle. "Seals, tertles, sammon, an so on: den, when you've cleared all de jelly-fish ourr'o de way—"

94

"*Dat* genrally takes ages," innerruptid de Gryphon.

"—you advance twice—"

"Each wid a lobster as a partner!" cried de Gryphon.

"Of course," de Mock Tertle said: "advance twice, set to partners—"

"—change lobsters, an retire in same order," continued de Gryphon.

"Den, you know," de Mock Tertle wenn on, "you trow de—"

"De lobsters!" shouted de Gryphon, wid a bound into de air.

"—as far out to sea as you can—"

"Swim after dem!" screamed de Gryphon.

"Tern a somersault in de sea!" cried de Mock Tertle caperin wildly about .

"Change lobsters again!" yelled de Gryphon at de top of its voice.

"Back to land again, an—dat's all de ferst figger," said de Mock Tertle, sunnly droppin iz voice; an de two creatchers, oo'd been jumpin about like mad tings all dis time, sat down again dead sad an quiet, an luwked at Alice.

"It muss be a dead custy dance," said Alice timidly.

"Would you like to see a birr'of it?" said de Mock Tertle.

"Yeah, I'd really love to," said Alice.

"Come ead, let's try de ferst figger!" said de Mock Tertle to de Gryphon. "We can do it widout lobsters, you know. Which shall sing?"

"Oh, *you* sing," said de Gryphon. "I've forgot de werds."

So dey began solemnly dancin round an round Alice, every now an den treadin on er toes when dey passed too close, an wavin deir fore-paws to mark de time while de Mock Tertle sang dis, very slowly an sadly:—

"Will you wawk a little faster?" said whitin to a snail,
"Der's a porpoise close be'ind us, an e's treadin on me tail.
See ow eagerly de lobsters an de tertles all advance!
Dey are waitin on de shingle—wo'n you come an join de
   dance?
      Will you, wo'n you, will you, wo'n you, will you join de
         dance?
      Will you, wo'n you, will you, wo'n you, wo'n you join de
         dance?

"You can really ave no notion ow delightful it will be,
When dey take us up an trow us, de lobsters, out to sea!"
But de snail replied "Too far, too far!" an gave a luwk
*   askance*
Said e tanked de whitin kinely, burr'e would not join de
*   dance,*
*   Would not, could not, would not. could not, would not join*
*   de dance.*
*   Would not, could not, would not, could not, could not join*
*   de dance.*

"What marrers irr'ow far we go?" iz scaly friend replied.
"Der is anudder shore, you know, upon de udder side.
De ferder off from England de nearer is to France—
Den tern not pale, belovèd snail, but come an join de dance.
*   Will you, wo'n you, will you, wo'n you, will you join de*
*   dance?*
*   Will you, wo'n you, will you, wo'n you, wo'n you join de*
*   dance?"*

"Tank you. It's a very intrestin dance to watch," said Alice, feelin dead glad darr'it was over at last: "An I do'n alf like dat curious song about de whitin!"

"Oh, as to de whitin," said de Mock Tertle, "dey—you've seen em, o course?"

"Yiss," said Alice, "I've offen seen em at dinn—" she checked erself astily.

"I do'n know where Dinn may be," said de Mock Tertle; "Burr'if you've seen dem so offen, o course you know what dey're like?"

"I believe so," Alice replied toughtfully. "Dey ave deir tails in deir mouts—an dey're all over crums."

"You're wrong about de crums," said de Mock Tertle: "Crums would all wash off in de sea. But dey *ave* deir tails in deir mouts; an de reason is—" ere de Mock Tertle yawned an shurr'iz eyes. "Tell er about de reason an all dat," e said to de Gryphon.

"De reason is," said de Gryphon, "dat dey *would* go wid de lobsters to de dance. So dey got trowed out to sea. So dey ad to fall a long way. So dey got deir tales in deir mowts. So dey could'n gerr'em out again. Dat's all."

"Ta, lar," said Alice, "It's dead intrestin. I never knew so much abourr'a whitin before."

"I can tell you more dan dat, if you like," said de Gryphon. "Do you know why it's called a whitin?"

"I never tought abourr'it," said Alice. "Why?"

"*It does de boots an shoes,*" de Gryphon replied very solemnly.

Alice was dead puzzled. "Does de boots and shoes!" she repeated in a wundrin tone.

"Why, Wharr'are *your* shoes done wid?" said de Gryphon. "I mean, what makes dem so shiny?"

Alice luwked down at dem, an considered a little before she gave er answer. "Dey're done wid blackin, I tink."

"Boots an shoes unner de sea," de Gryphon wenn on in a deep voice, "are done wid whitin. Now you know."

"An wharr'are dey made of?" Alice asked in a a tone o great curiosity.

"Soles an eels, o course," de Gryphon replied, radder impatiently. "Any shrimp could ave tole you dat."

"If I'd been de whitin," said Alice, oose toughts were still runnin on de song, "I'd ave said to de porpoise 'Ey you, naff off, pal! We do'n want *you* wid us!'"

"Dey were obliged to ave im wid dem," de Mock Tertle said. "No wise fish would go anywhere widout a porpoise."

"Would'n it really?" said Alice, in a tone o great suprise.

"Of course not," said de Mock Tertle. "Why, if a fish came to *me*, an tole me e was goin a jerney, I'd say 'Wid what porpoise?'"

"Do'n you mean 'perpose'?" said Alice.

"I mean wharr'I say," de Mock Tertle replied, in an offended tone. An de Gryphon added "Come ead, let's ear some o *your* adventchers."

"I could tell you me adventchers—beginnin from dis mornin," said Alice a little timidly; "burr'it's no use goin back to yisterdy, cause I was a diffrent person den."

"Explain all dat," said de Mock Tertle.

"No, no! De adventchers ferst," said de Gryphon in a impatient tone: "Explanations take such a awful time."

So Alice began tellin em er adventchers from de time when she ferst saw de White Rabbit. She was a little nervous abourr'it, just at ferst, de two creatchers got so close to er, one on each side, an opened deir eyes an mouts so very wide; but she gained couridge as she wenn on. Er lissners were dead quiet till she got to de part about er repeatin, *"You're ould, Faader William"*, to de Caterpilla, an de werds all comin diffrent, an den de Mock Tertle drew a long breath, an said "Dat's dead curious!"

"It's all abourr'as curious as it can be," said de Gryphon.

"Irr'all came diffrent!" de Mock Tertle repeated toughtfully. "I should like to ear er try an repeat sometin now. Tell er to begin." E luwked at de Gryphon as if e tought irr'ad some kind o authority over Alice.

"Stand up an repeat *'Tis de voice o de sluggard'*," said de Gryphon.

"De ain't alf fond o bossin you around, an makin you repeat lessins!" tought Alice. "I might just as well be still in school right now." Owever, she gorr'up, an began to repeat it, burr'er ead was so full o de Lobster-Quadrille, dat she din't ardly know what she was sayin; an de werds come dead queer indeed:—

"'Tis de voice o de Lobster: I eard im declare
"You ave baked me too brown, I muss sugar me air."
As a duck wid its eyelids, so e wid iz nose
Trims iz belt an iz buttins, an terns out iz toes.
When de sands are all dry, e's gay as a lark,
An will tawk in contemptuous tones o de shark:
But, when de tide rises an sharks are around,
Iz voice as a timid an tremulous sound."

"Dat's diffrent from what I used to say when I was a kid," said de Gryphon.

"Well, I never eard it before," said de Mock Tertle, "burr'it sounds a right load o rubbish."

Alice said nothin: she'd sat down wid er face in er ands, wundrin if anytin would *ever* appen in a natchural way again.

"I should like to ave it explained," said de Mock Tertle.

"She caan't explain it!" said de Gryphon astily. "Go on wid de next verse."

"But abourr'iz toes?" de Mock Tertle persisted. "Ow *could* e tern dem out wid iz nose, you know?"

"It's de ferst position in dancin," Alice said; but she was dead puzzled by de ole ting, an was dyin to change de subjeck.

"Go on wid de next verse," de Gryphon repeated. "It begins *'I passed by iz gardin'*."

Alice din't dare to disobey dough she felt sure i'would all come wrong, an she wenn on in a tremblin voice:—

> *"I passed by iz gardin, an marked, wid one eye,*
> *Ow de Owl an de Panther were sharin a pie:*
> *De Panther took pie-crust, an gravy, an meat,*
> *While de Owl ad de dish as its share o de treat.*
> *When de pie was all finished, de Owl, as a buwn,*
> *Was kinely permitted to pockit de spoon:*
> *While de Panther received knife an fork wid a growl,*
> *An concluded de banquet by—"*

"What *is* de use o repeatin all dat stuff?" De Mock Tertle innerrupted, "if you do'n explain irr'as you go on? It's by far de most confusin ting *I* ever eard!"

"Yiss, I tink you'd berrer leave off," said de Gryphon, an Alice was ony too glad to do so.

"Shall we try anudder figger o de Lobster-Quadrille?" de Gryphon wenn on. "Or would you like de Mock Tertle to sing you anudder song?"

"Oh, a song, please, if de Mock Tertle do'n mind," Alice replied, so eagerly dat de Gryphon said, in a radder offended tone, "Hm! No accountin for tastes! Sing er *'Tertle Soup'*, will you, me ould mate?"

De Mock Tertle sighed deeply, an began, in a voice choked wid sobs, to sing dis:—

Beautiful Soup, so rich an green,
Waitin in a ot chureen!
Oo for such dainties would not stoop?
Soup o de evenin, beautiful Soup!
Soup o de evenin, beautiful Soup!
  Beau-ootiful Soup!
  Beau-ootiful Soup!
Soo—oop o de e—e—evenin,
  Beautiful, beautiful Soup!

Beautiful Soup! Oo cares for fish,
Game, or any udder dish?
Oo would not give all else for two p
ennyworth ony o beautiful Soup?
Pennyworth ony o beautiful Soup?
  Beau-ootiful Soup!
  Beau-ootiful Soup!
Soo—oop o de e—e—evenin,
  Beautiful, beauti—FUL SOUP!"

"Chorus again!" cried de Gryphon an de Mock Tertle ad just begun to repeat it when a cry of "De trial's beginnin!" was eard in de distance.

"Come on!" cried de Gryphon an takin Alice by de and it urried off widout waitin for de end o de song.

"What trial is it?" Alice panted as she ran; but de Gryphon ony answered "Come on!" an ran de faster, while more an more faintly came, carried on de breeze dat follied dem, de melancholy werds:—

> *"Soo—oop o de e—e—evenin,*
>   *Beautiful, beautiful Soup!"*

CHAPTER XI

Oo Stole de Tarts?

De King an Queen of Arts were seated on deir trone when dey arrived, wid a load o people all round dem—all sorts o little berds an beasts, as well as de ole pack o cards: de Knave was standin before dem, in chains, wid a sodjer on each side to guard im; an near de King was de White Rabbit, wid a trumpit in one and, an a scroll o parchmint in de udder. Dead in de miggle o de cart was a table, wid a big dish o tarts on it: dey luwked so good, darr'it made Alice quite ungry to luwk at dem—"I wish dey'd get de trial done," she tought, "an and round de refreshmints!" But der seemed to be no chance o dis; so she began luwkin at everytin abourr'er to pass away de time.

Alice ad never been to court before, but she'd read abourr'em in buwks, an she was dead chuffed to find dat she knew de name o nearly everytin der. "Dat's de judge," she said to erself, "cause of iz big wig."

De judge, by de way, was de King; an, as e wore iz crown over de wig (luwk at de frontispiece if you wanna see ow e did it), e din't luwk arr'all comfy, an din't suit im arr'all.

"An dat's de jury-box," tought Alice; "an dose twelve creatchers," (she ad to say "creatchers", you see, cause some o dem were animals, an some were berds,) "I suppose dey're de jurors." She said dis last werd two or tree times over to erself, bein radder proud of it: for she tought, an rightly too, dat very few little gerls of er age knew de meanin of it arr'all. Owever, "jury-men" would ave done just as well.

De twelve jurors were all writin very busily on slates. "Wharr'are dey doin?" Alice whispered to de Gryphon. "Dey caan't ave nothin to put down yet, before de trial's begun."

"Dey're purrin down deir names," de Gryphon whispered in reply, "in case dey forget dem before de end o de trial."

"Stupid tings!" Alice began in a loud indignint voice; but she stopped erself astily, for de White Rabbit cried out "Silence in de court!" an de King purr'on iz specs an luwked round anxiously, to see oo was gabbin.

Alice could see, as well as if she were luwkin over deir shoulders, darr'all de jurors were writin down "Stupid tings!" on deir slates, an she could even make out dat one o dem din't know ow to spell "stupid", an dat e ad to ask iz neighbour to tell im. "A right mess deir slates'll be in, before de trial's over! tought Alice.

One o de jurors ad a pencil dat squeaked. Dis, o course, Alice could not stand, an she went round de court an got be'ind im, an very soon found an oppertchunity o takin irr'away. She did it so quickly dat de poor little juror (i'was Bill, de Lizard) could not make out arr'all wharr'ad become of it; so, after untin all over for it, e ad to write wid one finger for de rest o de day; an dis was'n much use, as it left no mark on de slate.

"Erald, read de accusation!" said de King.

On dis de White Rabbit blew tree blasts on de trumpit, an den unrolled de parchmint scroll, an read as follies:—

"De Queen of Arts, she made some tarts,
    All on a summer's day:
De Knave of Arts, e stole dose tarts
    An took dem quite away!"

"Consider your verdick," de King said to de jury.

"Not yet, not yet!" de White Rabbit astily innerrupted. "Der's a lot more to come before dat!"

"Call de ferst witness," said de King; an de White Rabbit blew tree blasts on de trumpit, an called out "Ferst witness!"

De ferst witness was de Atter. E came in wid a teacup in one and an a jam butty in de udder. "I beg pardon, your Majisty," e began, "for bringin dese in; burr'I ad'n quite finished me tea when I was sent for."

"You oughta ave finished," said de King. "When did you begin?"

De Atter luwked at de March Are, oo'd follied im into de court, arm-in-arm wid de Dormouse. "Fourteent o March, I *tink* i'was," e said.

"Fifteent," said de March Are.

"Sixteent," said de Dormouse.

"Write dat down," de King said to de jury; an de jury eagerly wrote down all tree dates on deir slates, an den added dem up, an reduced de answer to shillins an pence.

"Take off your at, " de King said to de Atter.

"Irr'ain't mine," said de Atter.

"*Stolen!*" de King exclaimed, ternin to de jury, oo instintly made a note o de fack.

"I keep dem to sell, de Atter added as an explanation. I've none o me own. I'm a atter."

Ere de Queen purr'on er specs, and began starin ard at de Atter, oo terned pale an fidgeted.

"Give your evidince," said de King, "an do'n be nervous, or I'll ave you exeecuted on de spot.

Dis din't seem to encouridge de witness arr'all: e kept shiftin from one foot to de udder, luwkin uneasily at de Queen, an in iz confusion e bit a large piece ourr'of iz teacup instead o de jam butty.

Just den Alice felt a very curious sensation, which puzzled er a lot until she made out wharr'it was: she was beginnin to grow larger again, an she tought at ferst she would gerr'up an leave de court; burr'on second toughts she decided to remain where she was as long as der was room for er.

"I wish you would'n squeeze so," said de Dormouse, oo was sittin next to er. "I can ardly breathe."

"I caan't elp it," said Alice very meekly: "I'm growin."

"You've no right to grow *ere*," said de Dormouse.

"Do'n tawk rubbish," said Alice more boldly: "You know you're growin too."

"Yiss, but *I* grow arr'a reasonable pace," said de Dormouse: "norr'in dat ridiculous fashion." An e gorr'up an crossed over to de udder side o de court.

All dis time de Queen ad never left off starin at de Atter, an, just as de Dormouse crossed de court, she said, to one o de officers o de court, "Bring me de list o de singers in de last concert!" on which de wretched Atter trembled so, darr'e shook off both iz shoes.

"Give your evidince," de King repeated angrily, "or I'll ave you exeecuted, whedder you're nervous or not."

"I'm a poor man, your Majisty," de Atter began, in a tremblin voice, "an I ad'n begun me tea—not above a week or so—an what wid de jam butty gerrin so smaller—an de twinklin o de tea—"

"De twinklin o *what?*" said de King.

"It *began* wid de tea," de Atter replied.

"Of course twinklin *begins* wid a T!" said de King sharply. "Do you take me for a dunce? Go on!"

"I'm a poor man," de Atter wenn on, "an most tings twinkled after dat—ony de March Are said—"

"I din't!" de March Are innerrupted in a big urry.

"You did!" said de Atter.

"I deny it!" said de March Are.

"E denies it," said de King: "leave out dat part."

"Well, arr'any rate, de Dormouse said—" de Atter wenn on, luwkin anxiously round

to see if e would deny it to; but de Dormouse denied nothin, bein fast asleep.

"After dat," continued de Atter, "I ad some more jam butties—"

"But what did de Dormouse say?" one o de jury asked.

"Darr'I caan't remember," said de Atter.

"You *muss* remember," remarked de King, "or I'll ave you exeecuted." De misrable Atter dropped iz teacup an jam butty, an went down on one knee. "I'm a poor man, your Majisty," e began.

"You're a *dead* poor *speaker*," said de King.

Ere one o de guinea-pigs cheered, an was immediately suppressed by de officers o de court. (As darr'is radder a ard werd, I'll just explain to you ow i'was done. Dey ad a large canvas bag, which tied up at de mout wid strings: into dis dey slipped de guinea-pig, ead ferst, an den sat upon it.)

"I'm glad I've seen dat done," tought Alice. "I've so offen read in de newspapers, at de end o trials, 'Der was some attempt at applause, which was immediately suppressed by de officers o de court,' an I never unnerstud wharr'it meant till now."

"If dat's all you know abourr'it, you may stand down," continued de King.

"I caan't go no lower," said de Atter: "I'm on de floor, as irr'is."

"Den you may *sit* down," de King replied.

Ere de udder guinea-pig cheered an was suppressed.

"Come, dat finishes de guinea-pigs!" tought Alice. "Now we shall gerr'on berrer."

"I'd radder finish me tea," said de Atter, wid an anxious luwk at de Queen, oo was readin de list o singers.

"You may go," said de King, an de Atter urriedly left de court, widout even waitin to purr'on iz shoes.

"—an just take iz ead off outside," de Queen added to one o de officers; but de Atter was out o sight before de officer could get to de door.

"Call de next witness!" said de King.

De next witness was de Duchess's cuwk. She carried de pepper-box in er and, an Alice guessed oo i'was, even before she gorr'in to de court, by de way people near de door began sneezin all at once.

"Give your evidince," said de King.

"Shan't," said de cuwk.

De King luwked anxiously at de White Rabbit, oo said, in a low voice, "Your Majisty muss cross-examine *dis* witness."

"Well, if I must, I must," de King said wid a melancholy air, an, after foldin iz arms an frownin at de cuwk till iz eyes were nearly out o sight, e said, in a deep voice, Wharr'are tarts made of?"

"Pepper mostly," said de cuwk.

"Treacle," said a sleepy voice be'ind er.

"Collar dat Dormouse!" de Queen shrieked out. "Be'ead dat Dormouse! Tern dat Dormouse ourr'o court! Suppress im! Pinch im! Off wid iz whiskers!"

For some minutes de ole court was in confusion, gerrin de Dormouse terned out, an, by de time dey'd settled down again, de cuwk ad done a bunk.

"Never mind!" said de King, wid an air o great relief. "Call de next witness." An e added, in an unnertone to de Queen, "Really, me love, *you* muss cross-examine de next witness. It quite makes me fore'ead ache!"

Alice watched de White Rabbit as e fumbled over de list, feelin dead curious to see what de next witness would be like, "—for dey aven't got much evidince *yet*," she said to erself. Imagine er suprise, when de White Rabbit read out, at de top of iz shrill little voice, de name "Alice!"

CHAPTER XII

Alice's Evidince

"*E*re!" cried Alice, quite forgettin in de flurry o de momint ow large she'd grown in de last few minutes, an she jumped up in such a urry dat she tipped over de jury-box wid de edge of er skirt, upsettin all de jurymen onto de eads o de crowd below, an der dey lay sprawlin about, remindin er a lot of a globe o goldfish she'd accidintly upset de week before.

"Oh, I *beg* your pardon!" she exclaimed in a tone o great dismay, an began pickin dem up again as quickly as she could, for de accidint o de goldfish kept runnin in er ead, an she ad a vague sorr'of idea dat dey muss be collected at once an put back into de jury-box, or dey would die.

"De trial caan't proceed," said de King, in a very grave voice, "until all de jurymen are back in deir proper places— *all*," e repeated wid great emphasis, luwkin ard arr'Alice as e said so.

Alice luwked at de jury-box, an saw dat, in er aste, she'd put de Lizard in ead downwerds, an de poor little ting was wavin its tail about in a melancholy way, bein quite unable to

112

move. She soon gorr'it ourr'again, an purr'it right; "not darr'it means much," she said to erself; "I should tink i'would be *quite* as much use in de trial one way up or de udder."

As soon as de jury ad recovered a bit from de shock o bein upset, an deir slates and pencils ad been found an anded back to dem, dey set to werk dead keen like to write out a istry o de accidint, all except de Lizard, oo seemed too much overcome to do anytin but sit wid its mout open, gozzin up to de roof o de court.

"What do you know about dis business?" de King said to Alice.

"Nothin," said Alice.

"Nothin *wharr'ever*?" persisted de King.

"Nothin wharr'ever," said Alice.

"Dat's dead importint," de King said, ternin to de jury. Dey were just beginnin to write dis down on deir slates, when de White Rabbit innerrupted: "*Un*importint, your Majisty means, o course," e said, in a very respeckful tone, but frownin an makin faces arr'im as e spoke.

"*Un*importint, o course I meant," de King astily said, an wenn on to imself in a unnertone, "importint—unimportint—unimportint—importint—" as if e were tryin which werd sounded best.

Some o de jury wrote it down "importint" an some "unimportint;" Alice could see dis, as she was near enough to luwk over deir slates; "burr'it do'n marrer a bit," she tought to erself.

At dis momint de King, oo'd been for some time busily writin in iz note-buwk, called out "Silence!", an read out from iz buwk, "*Rule Forty-two. All persons more dan a mile igh to leave de court.*"

Everybody luwked arr'Alice.

"I'm norr'a mile igh," said Alice.

"You are," said de King.

"Nearly two miles igh, " added de Queen.

"Well, I shan't go, arr'any rate," said Alice: "besides, dat's norr'a reglar rule: you just invented it now."

"It's de ouldest rule in de buwk," said de King.

"Den irr'oughta be Number One," said Alice.

De King terned pale, an shurr'iz note-buwk astily. "Consider your verdick," e said to de jury, in a low tremblin voice.

"Der's more evidince to come yet, please your Majisty," said de White Rabbit, jumpin up in a great urry: "Dis paper ad just been picked up."

"What's in it?" said de Queen.

"I aven't opened it yet," said de White Rabbit; "burr'it seems to be a lerrer, written by de prisner to—to somebody."

"It must ave been dat," said de King, "unless it was written to nobody, which is'n usual, you know."

"Oo's it directed to?" said one o de jurymen.

"Irr'is'n directed arr'all," said de White Rabbit: "in fack, der's nothin written on de *outside*." E unfolded de paper as e spoke, an added "Irr'is'n a lerrer, after all: it's a set o verses."

"Are dey in de prisner's andwritin?" asked anudder o de jurymen.

"No, dey're not," said de White Rabbit, "an dat's de queerest ting abourr'it." (De jury all luwked puzzled.)

"E must ave imitated somebody else's and," said de King. (De jury all brightened up again.)

"Please your Majisty," said de Knave, "I din't write it, an dey caan't prove darr'I did: der's no name signed at de end."

"If you din't sign it," said de King, "darr'ony makes de marrer werse. You must ave meant some mischief, or else you'd ave signed your name like an honest man."

Der was a genral clappin of ands at dis: i'was de ferst really clever ting de King ad said dat day.

"Dat *proves* iz guilt, o course," said de Queen: "so, off wid—"

"It do'n prove anytin o de sort!" said Alice. "Why, you do'n even know what dey're about!"

"Read dem," said de King.

De White Rabbit purr'on iz specs. "Where shall I begin, please your Majisty?" e asked.

"Begin at de beginnin," de King said, dead gravely, "an go on till you come to de end: den stop."

Der was dead silence in de court, while de White Rabbit read out dese verses:—

"Dey tole me you ad been to er,
*   An mentioned me to im:*
She gave me a good character,
*   But said I could not swim.*

E sent dem werd I ad'n gone
*   (We know it to be true):*
If she should push de marrer on,
*   What would become o you?*

I gave er one, dey gave im two,
*   You gave us tree or more;*
Dey all reterned from im to you,
*   Dough dey were mine before*

If I or she should chance to be
*   Involved in dis affair,*
E trusts to you to set dem free,
*   Exackly as we were.*

Me notion was dat you ad been
*   (Before she ad dis fit)*
An obsticle dat came between
*   Im, an ourselves, an it.*

Do'n lerr'im know she liked dem best,
*   For dis must ever be*
A secret, kept from all de rest,
*   Between yourself an me."*

"Dat's de most importint piece of evidince we've eard yet," said de King, rubbin iz ands; "so now let de jury—"

"If any one o dem can explain it" said Alice (she'd grown so large in de last few minutes dat she was'n a bit scared of innerruptin im), "I'll give im a tenner. *I* do'n believe der's an atom o meanin in it."

De jury all wrote down, on deir slates, "*She* do'n believe der's an atom o meanin in it," but none o dem ad a go at tryin to explain de paper.

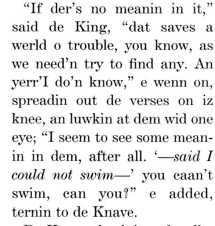

"If der's no meanin in it," said de King, "dat saves a werld o trouble, you know, as we need'n try to find any. An yerr'I do'n know," e wenn on, spreadin out de verses on iz knee, an luwkin at dem wid one eye; "I seem to see some meanin in dem, after all. '—*said I could not swim*—' you caan't swim, can you?" e added, ternin to de Knave.

De Knave shook iz ead sadly. "Do I luwk like it?" e said. (Which e certainly did not, bein made entirely o cardboard.)

"All right, so far," said de King; an e wenn on muttrin over de verses to imself: "'*We know it to be true*'—dat's de jury, o course—'*If she should push de marrer on*'—dat muss be de Queen—'*What would become o you?*'—What, indeed!—'*I gave er one, dey gave im two*'—why, dat muss be wharr'e did wid de tarts, you know—"

"Burr'it goes on '*dey all reterned from im to you*'," said Alice.

"Why, der dey are!" said de King, triumphantly, pointin to de tarts on de table. "Nothin can be clearer dan dat. Den again—'*before she ad dis fit*'—you never ad fits, me love, I tink?" e said to de Queen.

"Never!" said de Queen, furiously, trowin an inkstand at de Lizard as she spoke. (De unfortchunate little Bill ad left off writin on iz slate wid one finger, as e found it made no mark; burr'e now astily began again, usin de ink, dat was tricklin down iz face, as long as it lasted.)

"Den de werds do'n *fit* you," said de King, luwkin round de court wid a smile. Der was a dead silence.

"It's a pun!" de King added in a angry tone, an everybody laughed. "Let de jury consider deir verdick," de King said, for about de twenniet time dat day.

"No, no!" said de Queen. "Sentince ferst—verdick afterwerds."

"Stuff an nonsense!" said Alice loudly. "De idea of avin de sentince ferst!"

"Old your tongue!" said de Queen, ternin perple.

"I wo'n!" said Alice.

"'Off wid er ead!" de Queen shouted at de top of er voice. Nobody moved.

"Oo's boddered about *you?*" said Alice (she'd grown to er full size by dis time). "You're nothin burr'a pack o cards!"

At dis de ole pack rose up into de air, an came flyin down upon er; she gave a little scream, alf o fright an alf of anger, an tried to beat dem off, an found erself lyin on de bank, wid er ead in er sister's lap, oo was gently brushin away some dead leaves away darr'ad fluttered down from de trees upon er face.

"Wake up, Alice, love!" said er sister. "Why, wharr'a long sleep you've ad!"

"Oh, I've ad such a curious dream!" said Alice. An she tole er sister, as well as she could remember dem, all dese strange adventchers of ers dat you ave just been readin about; an, when she'd finished, er sister kissed er, an said "It *was* a curious dream, love, certainly; now go in for your tea: it's gerrin late." So Alice gorr'up an ran off, tinkin while she ran, as well as she might, wharr'a wunderful dream irr'ad been.

Burr'er sister sat still juss as she left er, leanin er ead on er and, watchin the settin sun, an tinkin o little Alice an all er wunderful Adventchers, till she too began dreamin in a sort o way, an dis was er dream:—

Ferst, she dreamed o little Alice erself: once again er diddy ands was grabbin arr'er knee, and er bright eager eyes were givin er de eyeball—she could ear de very tones of er gob, an see de oddball toss of er ead to keep back de wanderin air dat *would* allus get in er eyes—an still as she earwigged, or seemed to earwig, de ole place aroun er become alive wid de strange creatchers of er little sister's dream.

De long grass russled arr'er feet as de White Rabbit urried by—de frightened Mouse splashed iz way truw de neighbourin pool—she could ear de rattle o de teacups as de March Are an iz mates shared deir never-endin meal, and de shrill gob o de Queen orderin all de dead unlucky ones to be topped—once more de pig-baby was sneezin on de Duchess's knee, while de plates an dishes crashed roun it—once more de shriek o de Gryphon, de squeakin o de Lizard's slate-pencil, an de chokin o de suppressed guinea-pigs, filled de air, mixed up wid de distant sobs o de misry-gobbed Mock Tertle.

So she sat on, wid closed eyes, an alf believed erself in Wunderland, dough she knew she ony ad to open dem again, an all would change to dull reality—de grass would be ony russlin in de wind, an de pool ripplin to de wavin o de reeds—de rattlin teacups would change to tinklin sheep-bells, an de Queen's shrill cries to de gob o de shepherd boy—an de sneeze o de baby, de shriek o de Gryphon, an all de udder oddball noises, would change (she knew) to de confused clamour o de busy farm-yard—while de lowin o de cattle in de distance would take de place o de Mock Tertle's heavy sobs.

Lastly, she pitchured to erself ow dis same little sister of ers would, in de after-time, be erself a grown woman; an ow she would keep, truw all er riper years, de simple an lovin eart of er childhood; an ow she would gadder about er udder little kids, an make *deir* eyes bright an eager wid many a strange tale, peraps even wid de dream o Wunderland o long ago; an ow she would feel wid all deir simple sorrows, an find a pleasure in all deir simple joys, remembrin er own child-life, an de appy summers' days.

Alice's Adventures in Wonderland, by Lewis Carroll 2008

Through the Looking-Glass and What Alice Found There,
by Lewis Carroll 2009

A New Alice in the Old Wonderland,
by Anna Matlack Richards, 2009

New Adventures of Alice, by John Rae, 2010

Alice Through the Needle's Eye, by Gilbert Adair, 2012

Wonderland Revisited and the Games Alice Played There,
by Keith Sheppard, 2009

Alice's Adventures under Ground, by Lewis Carroll 2009

The Nursery "Alice", by Lewis Carroll 2010

The Hunting of the Snark, by Lewis Carroll 2010

The Haunting of the Snarkasbord, by Alison Tannenbaum,
Byron W. Sewell, Charlie Lovett, and August A. Imholtz, Jr, 2012

Snarkmaster, by Byron W. Sewell, 2012

In the Boojum Forest, by Byron W. Sewell, 2014

Murder by Boojum, by Byron W. Sewell, 2014

Alice's Adventures in Wonderland,
Retold in words of one Syllable by Mrs J. C. Gorham, 2010

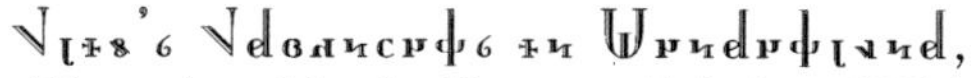

Ⱶⱡⱳⱷⱸ Ⱶⰺⱁⰺⱄⱌⱃⰼⱸ ⰺⱀ Ⱳⱃⱀⰼⱃⰼⱡⱴⱀⰼ,
Alice printed in the Deseret Alphabet, 2014

ⴹⰾ ⴹⰿⰽⴼⴲ � ⴹⰮⰽⴴⴼⴸ⵫ⰾⵏⴼⴸⴲ ⴹⴴⴸ ⴹⴲ ⴸⰮⴵⴹⰾ ⴹⴲⴸⰮ,
Alice printed in the Ewellic Alphabet, 2013

ˈÆlɪsɪz Əd'ventʃəz ɪn ˈWʌndə,lænd,
Alice printed in the International Phonetic Alphabet, 2014

Alis'z Advenčrz in Wundrland,
Alice printed in the Ñspel orthography, 2015

ᵒ.Ꮮ᙭Ꮯ⌐⌐Ꮣ⌐ ᵒ.⌐Ꭰᵒ∷⌐ᎺᔆᵒᵒⱢ⌐Ꮣ ᙭Ꮊ ᙭᙭Ꮊ⌐Ꮊ⌐,
Ꮮ ᵒ. ⱢⱢ Ꮣ, *Alice* printed in the Nyctographic Square Alphabet, 2011

ᴊᴄɪᔆ'ɪꜱ ɪʅʅɪᵒʅʞɔꜱ ɪɪ ·ɟʅɪ̣ᴅᴄɪɪ̣ʅ,
Alice printed in the Shaw Alphabet, 2013

ALISIZ ADVENƆ꒯RZ IN WUNDRLAND,
Alice printed in the Unifon Alphabet, 2014

Elucidating Alice: A Textual Commentary on *Alice's Adventures in Wonderland*, by Selwyn Goodacre, 2015

Behind the Looking-Glass: Reflections on the Myth of Lewis Carroll, by Sherry L. Ackerman, 2012

Clara in Blunderland, by Caroline Lewis, 2010

Lost in Blunderland: The further adventures of Clara, by Caroline Lewis, 2010

John Bull's Adventures in the Fiscal Wonderland, by Charles Geake, 2010

The Westminster Alice, by H. H. Munro (Saki), 2010

Alice in Blunderland: An Iridescent Dream, by John Kendrick Bangs, 2010

Rollo in Emblemland, by J. K. Bangs & C. R. Macauley, 2010

Gladys in Grammarland, by Audrey Mayhew Allen, 2010

Alice's Adventures in Pictureland,
by Florence Adèle Evans, 2011

Eileen's Adventures in Wordland, by Zillah K. Macdonald, 2010

Phyllis in Piskie-land, by J. Henry Harris, 2012

Alice in Beeland, by Lillian Elizabeth Roy, 2012

The Admiral's Caravan, by Charles Edward Carryl, 2010

Davy and the Goblin, by Charles Edward Carryl, 2010

Alix's Adventures in Wonderland:
Lewis Carroll's Nightmare, by Byron W. Sewell, 2011

Aloþk's Adventures in Goatland, by Byron W. Sewell, 2011

Alice's Bad Hair Day in Wonderland,
by Byron W. Sewell, 2012

The Carrollian Tales of Inspector Spectre,
by Byron W. Sewell, 2011

Alice's Adventures in An Appalachian Wonderland,
Alice in Appalachian English, 2012

Alice tu Vãsilia ti Ciudii, *Alice* in Aromanian, 2015

Алесіны прыгоды ў Цудазем'і, *Alice* in Belarusian, 2013

Ahlice's Aveenturs in Wunderlaant,
Alice in Border Scots, 2015

Alice's Mishanters in e Land o Farlies,
Alice in Caithness Scots, 2014

Crystal's Adventures in A Cockney Wonderland,
Alice in Cockney Rhyming Slang, 2015

Aventurs Alys in Pow an Anethow, *Alice* in Cornish, 2015

Alice's Ventures in Wunderland, *Alice* in Cornu-English, 2015

Alices Hændelser i Vidunderlandet, *Alice* in Danish, 2015

La Aventuroj de Alicio en Mirlando,
Alice in Esperanto, by E. L. Kearney, 2009

La Aventuroj de Alico en Mirlando,
Alice in Esperanto, by Donald Broadribb, 2012

Trans la Spegulo kaj kion Alico trovis tie,
Looking-Glass in Esperanto, by Donald Broadribb, 2012

Les Aventures d'Alice au pays des merveilles,
Alice in French, 2010

Alice's Abenteuer im Wunderland, *Alice* in German, 2010

Alice's Adventirs in Wunnerlaun,
Alice in Glaswegian Scots, 2014

Balþos Gadedeis Aþalhaidais in Sildaleikalanda,
Alice in Gothic, 2015

Nā Hana Kupanaha a ʻĀleka ma ka ʻĀina Kamahaʻo,
Alice in Hawaiian, 2012

Ma Loko o ke Aniani Kū a me ka Mea i Loaʻa iā ʻĀleka ma
Laila, *Looking-Glass* in Hawaiian, 2012

Aliz kalandjai Csodaországban, *Alice* in Hungarian, 2013

Eachtraí Eilíse i dTír na nIontas,
Alice in Irish, by Nicholas Williams, 2007

Lastall den Scáthán agus a bhFuair Eilís Ann Roimpi,
Looking-Glass in Irish, by Nicholas Williams, 2009

Eachtra Eibhlís i dTír na nIontas,
Alice in Irish, by Pádraig Ó Cadhla, 2015

Le Avventure di Alice nel Paese delle Meraviglie,
Alice in Italian, 2010

L's Aventuthes d'Alice en Êmèrvil'lie, *Alice* in Jèrriais, 2012

L'Travèrs du Mitheux et chein qu'Alice y démuchit,
Looking-Glass in Jèrriais, 2012

Las Aventuras de Alisia en el Paiz de las Maraviyas,
Alice in Ladino, 2014

Alisis pīdzeivuojumi Breinumu zemē, *Alice* in Latgalian, 2015

Alicia in Terra Mirabili, *Alice* in Latin, 2011

Aliciae per Speculum Trānsitus (Quaeque Ibi Invēnit),
Looking-Glass in Latin, 2014

Alisa-ney Aventuras in Divalanda,
Alice in Lingua de Planeta (Lidepla), 2014

La aventuras de Alisia en la pais de mervelias,
Alice in Lingua Franca Nova, 2012

Alice ehr Eventüürn in't Wunnerland,
Alice in Low German, 2010

Contoyrtyssyn Ealish ayns Çheer ny Yindyssyn,
Alice in Manx, 2010

Ko ngā Takahanga i a Ārihi i te Ao Mīharo,
Alice in Māori, 2015

Dee Erläwnisse von Alice em Wundalaund,
Alice in Mennonite Low German, 2012

The Aventures of Alys in Wondyr Lond,
Alice in Middle English, 2013

L'Aventuros de Alis in Marvoland, *Alice* in Neo, 2013

Ailice's Anters in Ferlielann, *Alice* in North-East Scots, 2012

Æðelgýðe Ellendæda on Wundorlande,
Alice in Old English, 2015

Die Lissel ehr Erlebnisse im Wunnerland,
Alice in Palantine German, 2013

Соня въ царствѣ дива: Sonja in a Kingdom of Wonder,
Alice in Russian, 2013

Ia Aventures as Alice in Daumsenland,
Alice in Sambahsa, 2013

'O Tāfaoga a 'Ālise i le Nu'u o Mea Ofoofogia,
Alice in Samoan, 2013

Eachdraidh Ealasaid ann an Tìr nan Iongantas,
Alice in Scottish Gaelic, 2012

Alice's Adventchers in Wunderland, *Alice* in Scouse, 2015

Alice's Adventirs in Wonderlaand, *Alice* in Shetland Scots, 2012

Alice Munyika Yamashiripiti, *Alice* in Shona, 2015

Ailice's Aventurs in Wunnerland,
Alice in Southeast Central Scots, 2011

Alices Äventyr i Sagolandet, *Alice* in Swedish, 2010

Ailis's Anterins i the Laun o Ferlies,
Alice in Synthetic Scots, 2013

'Alisi 'i he Fonua 'o e Fakaofo', *Alice* in Tongan, 2014

Alice's Carrànts in Wunnerlan, *Alice* in Ulster Scots, 2013

Der Alice ihre Obmteier im Wunderlaund,
Alice in Viennese German, 2012

Ventürs jiela Lälid in Stunalän, *Alice* in Volapük, 2015

Lès-avirètes da Alice ô payis dès mèrvèyes,
Alice in Walloon, 2012

Anturiaethau Alys yng Ngwlad Hud, *Alice* in Welsh, 2010

I Avventur de Alìs ind el Paes di Meravili,
Alice in Western Lombard, 2015

Alison's Jants in Ferlieland, *Alice* in West-Central Scots, 2014

Di Avantures fun Alis in Vunderland, *Alice* in Yiddish, 2015

U-Alice Ezweni Lezimanga, *Alice* in Zulu, 2014

Lightning Source UK Ltd.
Milton Keynes UK
UKOW04f0940240715

255763UK00001B/29/P